DEATH
BY
HANGING BASKET

Daphne Neville

ISBN: 978-0-244-84041-9

PublishNation
www.publishnation.co.uk

Other Titles by This Author

Chapter One

Twin sisters, Hetty and Lottie, stood up simultaneously and turned their heads as the opening notes of the *Bridal Chorus* rang out through the ancient village church. They and several other ladies in the congregation, gasped as the bride emerged through the arched doorway and slowly walked up the aisle on the arm of her father followed by four bridesmaids dressed in cobalt blue. Waiting on the chancel step was the bride's husband-to-be, the church's own vicar, Vicar Sam and with him, his best man, an old school friend from up-country with whom he had kept in touch over the years.

The wedding ceremony's readings, poems and hymns preached of morality, sincerity and love, mixed with a large dose of humour. At times the guests laughed, at times they cried and when the couple walked back down the aisle, arm in arm as man and wife there was a loud round of applause. While outside beneath the blue sky the church bells rang out across the village in celebration.

After the service which was taken by the vicar of a neighbouring parish, the wedding guests congregated around the churchyard, phones raised as they joined the photographer by taking pictures of the bridal party in front of the medieval porch. Warmed by the glorious June sunshine, delighted by the lovely wedding and the wonderful atmosphere, guests chatted and laughed, happy to see their young vicar married at last.

As the newlyweds left the churchyard and walked beneath the lichgate, Lottie reached in her handbag for a box of confetti and then she and other guests showered Vicar Sam and Martha, his bride as they stepped down onto the pavement. The groom, and his bride dressed in a full length, ivory satin gown, then walked along the street and down to the beach so that the photographer could take photographs of them beside the sea. While the pictures were being taken, the guests made their way to Pentrillick House for the reception. Martha had originally planned that the Crown and Anchor, the village's pub, be the venue for the reception but that was not possible because it had recently changed hands and the new owners had closed the business to make extensive alterations. It was therefore suggested by a member of Vicar Sam's congregation that they hold the reception instead at Pentrillick House. The owners, Tristen and Samantha Liddicott-Treen were keen to extend the use of their home to hold events such as weddings, and Emma, their new Events Manager, was doing a sterling job at organising such occasions.

The area designated for wedding receptions was a cordoned off stretch of grass down by the far end of the lake where a large white marquee owned by Pentrillick House remained erected for use during the summer months.

"What an idyllic spot to hold a wedding reception," said Hetty, as she and her contemporaries sat on benches overlooking the lake, glasses of wine in hand while they awaited the arrival of the bride and groom.

"It is and it's so nice to relax now. I thought we were going to be late for the wedding, you see," confessed Kitty. "Ten minutes before we wanted to leave, would you believe, some bloke turned up doing surveys. I didn't want to turn him away because he was so charming and polite. Anyway we made it in the nick of time, thank goodness."

Hetty crossed her legs and removed a leaf stuck on the sole of her shoe. "Just as well as it would've been a rum do if you'd not been there to play the organ when the bride arrived at the church."

The wedding feast was basic as neither Martha nor Sam wanted a big fuss or unnecessary waste. All of the food was produced or grown in Cornwall, as were the flowers on the tables and in the bride's bouquet.

Once everyone was present they made their way into the marquee where they ate around octagonal tables. They were entertained by a local band who played quietly on a raised platform where guests would later be invited to dance. When the three courses were finished and the speeches over many wandered back outside to enjoy the June sunshine.

"What do you think of the vicar?" Lottie asked.

Hetty frowned. "Do you mean Sam or the one who took the service?"

"The one who took the service of course and who will be our vicar while Sam and Martha are away."

"I thought he was alright. He had a gentle calming voice."

Tommy Thomas chuckled. "Too gentle. I think he might well lull me off to sleep in church tomorrow morning."

His wife, Kitty tutted but refrained from commenting. Instead she nodded in the direction of Lottie's grandson, Zac who was sitting on the grass with his girlfriend Emma, the aforementioned events manager at Pentrillick House. "Do you think they'll ever get married?"

Lottie removed her hat and placed it on her lap. "I'd like to think so but I get the impression that a lot of youngsters these days don't seem to bother."

"And when they do get wed it doesn't seem to last," commented Hetty, "but as regards Zac and Emma, they're both still very young so there's plenty of time yet."

"How old is Zac now?" Kitty asked.

"Nineteen and I believe Emma is twenty."

"Oh to be so young," Kitty was wistful.

"And how does your Zac like plumbing?" Tommy was more pragmatic.

"He loves it," enthused Lottie, "his mum told us he never moans about going to work."

"Not surprised," chuckled Hetty, "Sid is a great laugh and Zac's very lucky to have someone like him to learn the trade from."

In the early evening, Vicar Sam and his bride said goodbye to their guests and left for Bristol where they were to stay overnight in a hotel before their flight to Italy the following morning. Everyone went out to wave them on their journey and watched as the car drove out of the grounds with 'just married' written in spray paint on a card attached to the boot and tin cans trailing from the bumper.

After the departure of the newlyweds, a second band began to play and their vibrant, rhythmical music soon enticed guests to take to the raised platform to dance. Those who felt their dancing days were a thing of the past sat outside the marquee chatting in the early evening sunshine or walked around the perimeter of the lake enjoying the peace and tranquillity.

As the light faded a fireworks display lit the darkening sky and by midnight all had returned to their homes leaving the grounds to nocturnal creatures and scavengers hunting for scraps of food.

As they left church the following morning, Lottie scooped up a handful of rose petals used as confetti to shower the bride and groom. Wanting a souvenir of the previous day, she slipped them into her pocket and then walked with Hetty beneath the lichgate and out onto the pavement. By the bus stop they paused to look to where a new wooden bench stood alongside the church's boundary wall. Hetty admired its shape and couldn't resist the temptation to try it for comfort. "I think putting a bench here is an excellent idea and so ten out of ten to whoever thought of it. I meant to say so yesterday when we left the church after the wedding but didn't because Debbie was telling us how she was chatting to Alison Rowe before the service and that Ashley is writing a book."

Lottie sat down beside her sister. "Ashley writing a book, whatever next. I do hope he does though because I should love to read it."

"Hmm, it'll certainly be interesting especially if he uses some of the incidents he witnessed over his years in the pub. As he's threatened to do."

"Well if he does he'll have to change the names, won't he? Or in some cases he'll be done for libel."

"Yes, but I don't think he will. I reckon he's just trying to wind people up and the book is more likely to be non-fiction and about one of his hobbies, you know cricket or golf. After all he did like to pull the legs of his customers and that's why he was so popular."

Lottie sighed. "And so was Alison. The Crown and Anchor won't be the same when it opens up again without them behind the bar. We've never known any publicans here other than them, have we?"

"No, but then we have only known the village for three years. I agree though. It won't be the same and I'm not sure I like the new couple. Not that I've ever spoken to them, in fact I've only even seen them once and that was when they were outside the pub talking to one of the builders."

"Same with me, Het, but they've certainly put the cat amongst the pigeons with the alterations they're making to the old place. I liked it as it was so I'm not sure whether or not I approve of making it bigger."

"It's the resistance to change, I suppose. We'll probably like it when we get used to it. I just hope it doesn't take too long. I miss popping in for a drink after bingo and the Hotel bar just isn't the same."

5

As they sat chatting, a Range Rover pulled up beside Sea View Cottage, a detached house situated on the opposite side of the road. From it stepped a young couple who walked towards the front door of the cottage carrying bags of shopping.

Hetty craned her neck to get a better view. "They must be the new tenants. You know, the ones Kitty was telling us about. She said they've got the place on a long let and I know she told us their names but for the life of me I can't remember either of them."

"Sophie and Ivor Shepherd. That's what they're called." Lottie watched as the couple went inside the cottage and closed the door. "Apparently, he's a paramedic and she's a dental nurse or is it the other way round? I can't remember."

Hetty slapped her thigh. "Shepherd, yes of course. When I first heard the name it made me think of Winnie the Pooh and on reflection, I think you were right first time. He's the paramedic and she's the dental nurse."

"Winnie the Pooh, but that was written by A A Milne, Het."

"Yes, I know but E H Shepherd drew the pictures. I still have my Winnie the Pooh books and look at them from time to time," Hetty sprang to her feet, "Anyway, let's go home, Lottie. I don't know about you but I'm longing for a coffee and a piece of that fruit cake you made on Friday."

Lottie stood up and straightened the skirt of her dress. "Yes, so am I and I intend to have a very lazy day today after all the excitement of the wedding yesterday. All that chatting and loud music quite wore me out."

Inside the Crown and Anchor, the new landlord, James Dale, a man in his late forties, looked over the pub's newly built extension and rubbed his hands with glee. It was Monday morning, he could see the lads' vans were back and parked on the field meaning they soon would be in to begin another week's work.

The extension to the pub was on the side of the existing building and covered the original car park. The ground floor work had not altered the layout of the bar, but had increased the size and seating capacity of the dining room and work area of the kitchen; it also included new toilets.

James walked up the stairs to a small landing where doors led into three new en-suite guest rooms, each with a different aspect. He went into the first and touched the walls. The new plaster had dried to a pretty pale pink making the room look bright and airy. The window looked to the west and out over a field adjoining the old boundary of the pub. He and his wife Ella had purchased the field from a local farmer for use as a new car park, a children's playground, gardens and an area for camping.

As four people emerged from caravans on the field, James opened the window. "Good morning, lads. Hope you had a good journey back." He waved his hands towards the sky, "and what a beautiful day to begin a new week."

The four men acknowledged his greeting with nods and grunts.

"I'll be down in a minute to put the kettle on." He closed the window but before he went back downstairs, he returned to the landing and entered his favourite room with a south facing aspect out over the sea. He opened the window and, with hands resting on the sill, took in a deep breath of the clean, fresh air; he then looked to the beach below. The sea sparkled, the tide was out and because it was still early in the day, other than a few seagulls waddling across the sand, the beach was deserted. "Wonderful," muttered James, "What a location, perfect for a pub." He closed the window a very happy man. The work was coming on well and it was anticipated that by mid-July the premises would be ready to re-open. Just in time for the summer holiday season. Things couldn't get much better.

Chapter Two

In their first floor flat above the village's charity shop, Robert and Sally Oliver ate breakfast in the small dining room and gazed down onto the beach below. Aged in their mid to late sixties, they were retired and had moved to Pentrillick from Birmingham in early March. Being keen gardeners they would have preferred a house in Cornwall with garden front and back but as they also wanted a sea view and because their budget was limited it was not possible to have both. Therefore they decided to compromise and bought the small flat with its view of the sea and to feed their horticultural interest they planned to visit gardens open to the public at least once a week. However, that proved not to be necessary for luck was on their side when one day soon after they had arrived in the village, Robert saw in the post office window a notice for part-time workers to help in the gardens of Pentrillick House. They applied for and were given jobs.

The married couple loved their work in the prestigious grounds from the very first moment but when Sally was told that a bowling green was under construction behind the house she was ecstatic for bowls was her passion and she had been well known at her previous address for her expertise.

It was Emma, the events manager's idea to have a bowling green for her grandmother was a keen player and with a high proportion of Cornwall's residents being retired Emma thought it might prove a source of interest for them. The Liddicott-Treeens who owned Pentrillick House and its grounds agreed. The green was opened for business at the beginning of May, after which Sally moved from working in the gardens to the green where she was available to advise and help novice players learn a few tricks and manoeuvres.

Early on Monday evening, after he had finished work, showered and had a bite to eat, Sid, a jovial middle-aged plumber left his home in Honeysuckle Drive and walked through the village to the hotel for a pint or two of beer. He enjoyed the walk: after a day bending at work it was nice to stretch his legs and because the evening was fine and the sun was still shining he arrived at the hotel in good spirits. Sitting around a large table in the corner of the bar were four men who Sid knew to be the tradesmen working on the Crown and Anchor. Knowing they were congenial chaps he took his pint and asked if he might join them.

"How's the job coming along?" Sid asked, "I must say it's looking very impressive and I've heard several people saying complimentary things."

"It's coming on really well and we should have it all done on time, which is pleasing the governor," said Vince, the oldest of the four men, "I've finished plastering the upstairs rooms now and should have the downstairs done by the middle of next week, then I'll be starting on the wardrobes as I've already put the doors in."

"Wardrobes. Doors. So are you a chippy as well?"

"Yes, that was the first thing I learned to do when I left school. Plastering came later when I thought it might wise to have another string to my bow."

"Ah, that's interesting so which do you prefer?"

"Not really much to choose between them as there's job satisfaction with both. Plastering's mucky but seeing a newly plastered wall when it's dried never ceases to please me."

"Yes, I can understand that," Sid took a sip of his beer, "So, is it only you four left now?"

Leo tore open two packets of salt and vinegar crisps and placed them in the middle of the table. "Yes, the roofers went back to base last week and the brickies the week before that. Help yourself to crisps, lads."

Three hands took a small handful. Sid declined.

"And now have I got this right? You're doing the stone facing, Leo?"

"Yep. Spot on."

"And me too," said Max, "although Leo does the artistic bit and I'm just his general dogsbody."

"No that's not fair. You've put in quite a few stones on this job and made a damn good effort too."

Max beamed with pride. Sid meanwhile addressed the tall, slim man who sat at the opposite side of the table; he wore his long hair pulled back in a ponytail and his face, it seemed, was set in a permanent smile. "And I believe you're a plumber, Gavin, like myself."

"That's right. Went to college and learned the trade when I left school and have never done anything else."

"Is it something you enjoy?"

"I do, yes. Plenty of job satisfaction, especially an interesting project like the pub. It's a great location and I love being by the sea. Best job we've had for years."

Sid patted his stomach. "Well, at least you're the right shape for plumbing. I got a bit overweight a few years back and it made the bending and squeezing into small spaces damn near impossible. I've lost most of it now though."

Vince laughed. "That's never a problem with us plasterers; all that stretching and lugging around bags of the stuff keeps us fit."

"Same with doing stone work," agreed Leo, "beats going to the gym and lifting weights."

"So what do you think of our village pub?" Sid asked.

"Well, that's a tricky one," laughed Vince, "I mean, with us working on it means it's closed for business so we can't sample its wares. And don't get me wrong, this hotel is nice enough and I don't know about the others, but I feel a bit out of place. You know, wouldn't dare come in for a pint after work without getting spruced up first."

"Yeah, I agree, it is a bit of a bugger," said Max, "but we've got into a routine now and so it's not too bad."

Leo raised his glass. "And the beer's good so it's worth the effort."

"But it's only for five nights a week anyway, isn't it," said Sid, "because you go home at the weekends."

Vince shook his head. "Actually, it's only four nights. We drive home after work on Friday and then come back early on Monday morning. I was tempted at first to go home every night but it seemed a dreadful waste of time and fuel, and to be fair to James the caravans are very comfy, aren't they, lads?"

Leo, Gavin and Max nodded.

"Especially now there are only four of us left because we've each got a van to ourselves."

"Tell me about the Dales. I mean, you lot probably know them better than anyone else in the village. What are they like?" Sid asked.

"No complaints as far as I'm concerned," said Max, "they treat us well. There's no shortage of tea, coffee and cake and they usually provide us with lunch as well."

Vince agreed. "Yes, they're nice and easy going. I've never had reason to dislike them and we don't see much of Ella anyway. I reckon James is in charge of the building side and she'll take over when it comes to the decorating."

Leo tipped the last of the crisps into his hand. "Yes, and that's because she's very creative and I don't know whether

11

you know, Sid, but she's a great artist too. We've seen some of her paintings and they're top-notch."

"I didn't know that," acknowledged Sid, "so what does she paint?"

"Seascapes, landscapes, flowers; all sorts really," said Leo.

Max frowned. "I don't think she does portraits though, does she? I'm sure James said she's not very good when it comes to hands or perhaps I dreamt it."

"No, you're right," Vince looked around as someone closed a window, "she's rubbish at hands."

"Well, with any luck we'll get to see some of her work when the pub opens," Sid hoped it would be a lot better than the piece of modern art on the wall behind Gavin.

Vince nodded. "You will. I know she's intending to put a couple in the dining room and I daresay she'll find room in the bar as well."

Gavin drained his glass and stood up. "They're well worth seeing. Anyway, my round now. Same again everyone and that includes you, Sid?"

Chapter Three

Emma, enthusiastic from the very first day in her new job as the events manager at Pentrillick House, had suggested to her employers in early January that it might be a nice idea to hold a Pentrillick in Bloom competition for residents of the village to enter. Justin Liddicott-Treen thought it an excellent idea and said that he would be happy to provide prize money for the winners. His wife, Samantha agreed so posters were printed and pinned up in various locations throughout the village. Application forms were made available in the post office and at Pentrillick House. There were four categories, shop fronts and business premises, large front gardens, small front gardens, and for those without any front garden at all, a category for displays of pots, tubs, window boxes and hanging baskets. The rules were simple. Any type of flower or vegetable was permitted but all hanging baskets, pots, tubs and window boxes must be the work of the competitor and not to have been constructed professionally. Likewise, front gardens, large and small had to be the work of the entrants.

News of the competition was met by the residents with great enthusiasm and packets of seeds sold quickly in the village shop and local supermarkets as everyone was keen to do his or her best to enhance the look of the village and possibly win a prize.

Hetty and Lottie who had a small front garden had filled their south facing window sills with seed trays back in March, determined to make sure they had plenty of plants to fill all the gaps and make a colourful display. Once the seeds had germinated they had pricked out the young seedlings and put them into the greenhouse. By the end of April the young plants were a good size and ready to be hardened off. Then in early May the sisters had planted them out with a little more care and creativity than in previous years.

Meanwhile, at the Old Bakehouse, Lottie's daughter-in-law, Sandra, who did not have a front garden, had filled tubs and window boxes with perennials and annuals grown from seed which she had estimated would be in full flower by the end of July when the judging was due to take place. The house was on the corner of the main street and Goose Lane so she reasoned that her display, if all went well, would be striking to anyone walking or driving through the village.

Not to be outdone, her husband, Bill, had insisted he also take part. From the supermarket where he worked he bought a hanging basket, a bracket, and three yellow flowering plants which he bedded in multi-purpose compost. His finishing touch was a spindly plant of variegated ivy.

Sandra had looked on in disbelief as Bill hung the basket on the bracket he had fixed on the wall beside the front door of their house.

"You really need two baskets. It looks off-balance with just one."

Bill stepped from the pavement and onto the road to get a better look. "No, it doesn't. One's fine, it's all about quality not quantity, Sandra."

"Humph. Well talking of quantity, is that all you're going to put in? I mean, as pretty as the little flowers are, it looks a bit sparse, Bill."

"Maybe but I reckon these little beauties will thicken up before long. You wait and see."

"I doubt it and even if they do, there are very few buds so they'll have long passed their best by the end of July when the judging takes place. Apart from that you really need more colour, Bill. Yellow on its own just isn't eye catching enough."

"I chose yellow because it matches the front door and I don't want another colour as well. Besides there is another colour. The leaves are green and so is the ivy."

"But…"

Bill wagged his finger at his wife. "I think you're jealous of my creation, Sandra. But just you wait and see. My hanging basket will be the talk of the village."

Sandra gave up.

Every morning before he went to work, Bill had faithfully watered his hanging basket and removed any dead or faded flowers and leaves. However, six weeks after he had created his offering the plants still looked much as they had on that first day. Nevertheless, he was not disheartened by the lack of progress and spoke a few words of encouragement to the little plants every time he entered or left the house; after all if it was acceptable for a future king to do so then it was fine for him to do likewise.

On Friday morning when he stepped out into the street with watering can in hand, he looked up at the bracket and his jaw dropped in disbelief. The bracket was empty. His basket was no longer there. With face like thunder he returned indoors, slamming the watering can down on the dining room table which caused water to splash onto the cloth. "Okay," he roared to the children as they came down the stairs for breakfast, "what have you done with it?"

Zac yawned. "Done what with what?"

"My hanging basket. It's missing."

Vicki giggled. "Probably someone was jealous and so they've nicked it to add to their own display."

"Don't mock my efforts, young lady."

"What's the matter? What's all the shouting about? And who has spilled water on the clean tablecloth? I only put it on this morning." Sandra had entered the room, mug of coffee in hand.

"Someone has hidden or stolen my hanging basket."

Sandra put down her coffee mug beside the watering can. "Don't be silly, Bill, why would anyone do that?" She opened the door and stepped out onto the pavement. "Oh, dear, wherever can it be?" She walked to the corner of the house and peeped into Goose Lane, "My tubs and window boxes are still here, I've just counted them."

"I daresay it was some drunk on his way back from the hotel," reasoned Vicki's twin sister Kate, "and he's probably chucked it in someone's front garden for a lark."

Bill pulled his phone from his pocket. "I'm ringing the police."

Sandra snatched it from his hands. "No, Bill, at least not yet. First of all wait and see if anyone else in the village has had theirs taken because if it's just yours it'd be a dreadful waste of police time: they're over-stretched as it is."

Inside Sea View Cottage, Ivor Shepherd prepared breakfast while his wife, Sophie hung out the washing. When he went to the fridge for eggs, he found only one in the box.

"Damn," he muttered, "I meant to get some on my way home from work yesterday but clean forgot." He walked through the conservatory at the back of the house and called to his wife. "Just popping to the shop to get half a dozen eggs, Soph. Be back in a jiffy."

Sophie looked at her watch. "Will they be open yet? It's not quite eight so you might be unlucky."

"Good point but I should think they'll open up at eight. I'll pop along and see anyway as it's no distance from here but if I'm unlucky we'll have to share the one poached egg."

"A bit like our student days." Sophie smiled, took a hand towel from her laundry basket and shook it before she pegged it onto the line.

Ivor chuckled. "Yeah, those were the days, weren't they? Anyway I'm gone now. See you in a tick."

He left the house by the front door and whistled as he stepped out onto the pavement. He took in a deep breath as he closed the garden gate; the air felt fresh, birds sang in the trees, the street was quiet with very little traffic and no pedestrians were visible on the pavements. He stretched his arms, happy to embrace another day.

As he strode past a bungalow with an overgrown front garden, he heard the church clock strike eight and instinctively he looked towards the tower where its large white face glowed in the morning sun beneath the cloudless blue sky. Overwhelmed by the delights of the morning, Ivor felt that all was well with the world and that moving to Pentrillick was one of best things he had ever done in his life, along with marrying Sophie of course. However the feel-good factor promptly faded when his eyes fell back to ground level and he spotted something unusual in the graveyard. Just visible over the top of the church's front boundary wall, a pair of feet wearing grey trainers leaned against a tombstone. Wondering if perhaps someone had fallen asleep there the previous night after a few too many in the hotel bar, he crossed the road and entered the churchyard beneath the lichgate.

"Wake up, lad," Ivor called, "you'll get a chill lying there."

There was no response and as he walked along the gravel path he saw that the feet were attached to legs wearing tight fitting jeans. He spoke again; there was no reaction, no reply and neither feet nor legs moved. When the rest of the body came into view, Ivor realised why. A young man lay sprawled across the grave of someone long departed; his upper body was twisted, his face was blue. On top of his head was an empty hanging basket and its chain was wrapped firmly around the young man's neck. Ivor knelt down and felt for a pulse. As he expected there was none. The man was stone cold. Quickly Ivor sprang to his feet, pulled his phone from his pocket and rang for the police and an ambulance. As he waited for the emergency services he saw a small heap of compost nearby and upturned yellow flowers with a strand of variegated ivy lying discarded amongst a patch of dandelion seed heads.

Meanwhile, further along the road on the field beside the Crown and Anchor, Vince, one of the tradesmen working on the pub, knocked on the door of a caravan, its curtains closed. "Wake up, Gav. You're late for work, son. You'll have the boss after you." There was no response. Vince knocked again. Still no response. He tried the door. It was unlocked and so he went inside. He walked from one end of the caravan to the other, but Gavin was not there.

Chapter Four

"Have you heard the latest?" Kitty Thomas panted when Hetty answered the front door of Primrose Cottage later that morning.

Hetty stepped aside to let Kitty in. "Latest. Latest what? We've heard nothing worth repeating. Having said that we did hear sirens this morning but thought nothing of it."

Lottie came out into the hallway. "Have you been running, Kitty? You sound out of breath."

Hetty looked at Kitty's feet, "And you're still wearing your slippers."

"Oh bother, so I am. But yes, I did run here and that's because I wanted to come and tell you what's just happened while it's still fresh in my mind. Not that I'm likely to forget." Kitty took in a deep breath to steady her shaky voice. "You see, Tommy's just got back from the shop and told me the latest news and it's not good. Not for Gavin Snow anyway."

"Gavin Snow. Who on earth is he?" Hetty closed the door.

"One of the tradesmen working in the pub. A plumber according to Tommy and he's been murdered."

"What," screeched Lottie, "Let's go in the kitchen and I'll make tea while you tell us all you know."

"Good idea. I need to sit down as my legs have turned to wobbly jelly."

"So, did this take place where they're living on the pub's new field?" Hetty pulled out a chair for Kitty at the kitchen table.

"Thank you, Het," Kitty sat down. "No, it didn't, it was the churchyard would you believe?"

"The churchyard!" Hetty grabbed the front of the sink to stop herself from falling.

"Yes, dreadful, isn't it? Ivor Shepherd, you know the paramedic staying at Sea View Cottage, he found him."

Lottie tutted as she reached over her sister's arm and filled the kettle. "Dear oh dear and in the churchyard too, is nothing sacred anymore?"

"Perhaps someone ought to contact Vicar Sam and tell him?" Hetty moved away from the sink.

Kitty shook her head. "Oh no, that would be most inconsiderate after all it's not every day that he gets to be on honeymoon. Besides, I'm told the temporary vicar is taking care of things and cooperating fully with the police."

Hetty reached for the biscuit tin and arranged a selection on a plate; she placed it on the table and then sat down opposite Kitty. "So how did the poor man die or is it not yet known?"

"Oh, it's known alright and that's the terrible thing about it. You see, he was throttled with the chain of a hanging basket."

"He was what!" Hetty exclaimed, "It goes from bad to worse."

"Yes, it does." Kitty's hands were still shaking.

"How does Tommy know all this?" Lottie asked.

Kitty took a tissue from her sleeve and mopped her brow. "Your next door neighbour, Ginny, was walking by the church on her way to open up the antiques shop this morning when Ivor was on the phone to the police. Concerned by the tone of his voice she went to see what was wrong. After that word got round and when Tess Dobson went into the post office for some stamps and heard about it she went straight off down the road to the antiques shop on pretence of wanting a chamber pot for her rubber plant and questioned Ginny to find out the latest. On the way back she called in at the post office to report her findings and that's why everyone there was in the know when Tommy went in for his paper."

"Good old Tess. What would we do without her?" Hetty, having recovered from the shock, took a rich tea biscuit from the plate and broke it in two.

"So did she learn anything more than what you've told us?" Lottie placed mugs of tea on the table and then sat down.

"Not really, the only other thing was that compost and yellow flowering plants which must have come from the hanging basket were lying in a heap quite near to where poor Gavin was found."

"Yellow flowering plants." The colour drained from Hetty's face as she reached for her mobile phone and rang Bill's number.

On Saturday morning, in the front garden of their home in Honeysuckle Drive, Bernie the Boatman and his wife Veronica put out garden furniture on the lawns along with tables and chairs borrowed from the village hall. They then sat back and awaited the arrival of villagers whom they hoped would attend their coffee morning to help raise money for much needed equipment for the newly formed playgroup.

Bernie was a man in his late fifties who made a living taking holiday makers and locals out to sea on fishing trips during the summer months. Veronica, was a few years younger and her garden was her pride and joy.

By eleven o'clock people began to arrive; some brought prizes for the raffle, others homemade cakes. By midday all seats on the lawn were taken, for since the villagers had no pub to frequent many were keen to attend an event where they might catch up with the latest gossip and especially news of the recent murder in the village.

"Your garden is looking lovely," commented Hetty to Veronica, "are you entering the Pentrillick in Bloom competition?"

, Veronica nodded as she re-filled Hetty's mug with coffee inside the kitchen. "Oh, definitely yes and it seems that everyone else in the village is too. In fact I've yet to come across anyone who isn't. Even Sid next door is thinking about it and when we went along to the garden centre the other day for some fuchsias, a chap we know who works there told us that they had sold out of plastic window boxes and were waiting another delivery."

"I'm not surprised: it's created a real buzz in the village and now you come to mention it, I can't say that I've spoken to anyone who isn't keen on the idea but then most in our circle of friends are enthusiastic gardeners anyway."

Outside on the lawns, Clara Bragg, a dark haired, tall, slim woman in her late thirties who was a cook at the care home in the village, slowly walked around the garden looking at the flower beds. She wore white flip-flops with silver trims and a short white dress which showed off her newly acquired suntan.

"Looking for inspiration?" Sandra joked.

"Humph. No need for that. What I don't know about gardening isn't worth knowing. I'll win this competition hands down."

Sandra, who also worked at the care home, was rather taken aback by her work colleague's boastful comments. "Which category will you be in then? We don't have a front garden at the Old Bakehouse so it'll all be down to tubs and so forth for us."

"Same with me. I have a stunning back garden which is the envy of my neighbours even though I've only been working on it for less than a year. Sadly the front door opens onto the street, which is the shame."

Sandra tried to recall being told where Clara lived but drew a blank. "So, whereabouts is your place? I'm sure you're not along the main street, are you?"

Clara shook her head. "No, I live in Church Row?"

"Church Row?"

"It's a small terrace of houses at the back of the church, would you believe? Mine's on the end. It's not very big but there's more than enough room for me."

"I see, anyway if you've no front garden we'll be in competition with each other." Sandra thought of Bill's erstwhile hanging basket, currently a murder weapon, and prayed its replacement would have more pizzazz.

"Well that told you," chuckled Hetty, as Sandra sat back down and repeated what Clara had said, "Bragg by name and brag by nature is that one. I hope she comes last."

Lottie tutted. "That's a bit harsh, Het. She probably really does have green fingers."

"Well, time will tell. But she needs to curb her bragging or she might find someone slips weed killer into her efforts."

"Oh, Het, you wouldn't do that, would you?"

"Of course not, but I'm just saying someone else might. Besides, having a small front garden we'll not be in the same category as her anyway, so she's not a threat."

"Oh no, of course not." Lottie heaved a sigh of relief.

"So, Sandra, do you know where Clara lived before she came to Pentrillick?"

"Camborne I believe. At least she used to work over that way somewhere because I remember hearing when I started at the care home that she was a cook in a pub there. She didn't like working nights though so when she saw the advert for a cook at the care home she applied for and got it. I'm told by the residents that her cooking is very good although I haven't sampled anything myself."

Hetty put down her empty coffee mug on the grass. "But surely your residents have meals in the evening too so she'd still have to work nights."

Sandra shook her head. "No, they have a hot meal at lunch time and then in the early evening have something light like soup or a sandwich which is prepared by whoever is on duty."

"I see, so I suppose you do it sometimes."

"Yes, quite often and we give the residents a choice so there are no complaints. I must admit I find preparing food quite enjoyable so I rather like the early evening shift."

"Does Clara only work lunch times then?"

"No, she does breakfast as well so she's there all morning."

"And I expect she moved here to the village to save travelling," reasoned Lottie.

"Yes, I believe so. Makes sense anyway."

"Out of curiosity how long ago was that?" Hetty watched as with coffee in hand Clara sat down at a table opposite to where Sid was talking to Bernie.

"Sometime last summer. I know she'd only been working at the care home for a few months when I started there."

"Why so many questions about Clara, Het?" Lottie was intrigued.

"No reason really. I just like to know who everyone is especially now there's a murderer in our midst."

"Oh, but that's silly. Gavin Snow was not a local so it's unlikely his life was taken by anyone from the village."

"No, I suppose not. Still pays to be vigilant."

"One thing we do know about Gavin's case though," said Sandra, "is that whoever the murderer was, he walked past our house on that fateful night."

Hetty leaned forwards. "Why, did you see something?"

Sandra chuckled, amused by the inquisitive nature of her husband's aunt. "No, of course not."

"Oh. So how do you know he walked past your house?"

"Because en route to the churchyard he must have pinched Bill's hanging basket."

"Of course. Silly me." Hetty glanced at the people gathered on the lawns, "I keep looking and hoping to see Tess walk in because she's bound to have the latest news but as yet she's not put in an appearance."

Sandra stood to get a coffee refill. "That's because she's working in Taffeta's Tea Shoppe all day today. I saw her going in there this morning when I was out taking the dog for a walk. She said she was really sorry she was going to miss coming here but she has to work today because Taffeta and her husband have gone to a wedding in Fowey."

"Damn, that's a shame."

"Talking of weddings, it's a week already today since Sam and Martha got married," said Lottie, "how time flies."

"So it is," Hetty tutted, "Poor Sam. Goodness knows what he'll say when he hears about the murder in his churchyard."

Last to arrive at the coffee morning were Sally and Robert Oliver who lived in the flat above the charity shop; they thought they'd pop in to support the event before they went to work at Pentrillick House in the afternoon. They were greeted warmly by Bernie and Veronica who had met the newcomers recently on the beach and discovered they all shared a passion for gardening.

"We've been thinking," said Sally, as Veronica poured them both mugs of coffee, "We've noticed there's a lot of enthusiasm in the village for the Pentrillick in Bloom competition so do you think there would be the same amount of interest for a gardening club? Nothing complicated, just somewhere for like-minded people to meet, chat and exchange ideas."

Veronica put down the coffee pot and her mouth formed a perfect O. "What a wonderful idea. I can't believe no-one has ever thought of it before. You can certainly count me in, and Bernie as well."

Chapter Five

On Sunday morning, Hetty and Lottie went to church. They had considered giving Sung Eucharist a miss since Vicar Sam was away on his honeymoon but realising by attending the service it would enable them to walk past the area where Gavin Snow had died and therefore, it would be foolhardy to miss the opportunity to weigh up the situation for themselves; for both were keen to learn as much as possible about the crime and its exact location in order to visualise how the attack might have taken place. As they expected the area was still cordoned off with police tape and Bill's hanging basket was no longer there. Its contents, however, were.

"Oh no," Lottie's mouth turned upside-down, "Bill would be so upset if he knew that his poor flowers were lying higgledy-piggledy amongst a heap of compost in a patch of dandelion seed heads. I mean, not long ago they were his pride and joy, although I could never see why."

Hetty glanced over her shoulder to see if there was anyone within earshot. "When we come out of church after the service perhaps we could pick them out of the compost, take them home and give them a new lease of life because if they're left there much longer they'll wither up and be past revitalising."

"It's a nice idea, Het, but a bit risky, don't you think? I mean, to get to them we'd have to slip under or over the police tape and then we might contaminate the crime scene."

"No, I'm sure we wouldn't. The police, forensics or whatever must have collected all the evidence they want by now. Anyway if we're subtle they'll never know it was us because we won't touch or leave fingerprints on anything other than the plants and we'll take them with us."

"I still think it's too risky, Het, especially in broad daylight. I mean, this wall borders the pavement so anyone walking by would see us. What's more, the vicar always stands outside the church door after the service and chats to his flock as they leave so it would look highly suspicious if we were to hang around here especially near the scene of the crime."

"You're right, in which case we'll come back tonight after dark. We won't need a torch though because the streetlamp will provide sufficient light."

On Sunday afternoon, Robert Oliver went out with Bernie the Boatman and a few others on a fishing trip where he hoped to get a mackerel or two for supper. The weather was fine and the sea was flat calm as they left the shore and chugged along the coast towards Mount's Bay.

"The village looks totally different when seen from the sea," said Robert who sat beside Bernie at the boat's rudder, "Even our flat. If I'm honest I wouldn't have recognised it at all were it not for the fact it's a few doors away from the pub and that's only recognisable because of its sun terrace."

"Everyone says that," said Bernie, "even people who have known the village for years."

Robert took a flask from his bag. "Fancy a coffee? I've got two cups."

"Thank you, but no. I like to limit myself to no more than two a day and I've already had three."

Robert chuckled and poured coffee for himself. "So how long have you been living here, Bernie?"

"Since I was a boy. Well, actually since I was a baby. I've been here all my life you see."

"And Veronica?"

"No, she comes from St. Ives. We met many summers ago when I went over there one weekend with some mates. She was a student and working in one of the pubs and I was a trainee mechanic back then. That's what got me interested in boats. Messing around with engines."

"I see, and have you lived at Honeysuckle Drive ever since you got married?"

"No, we rented one of the small cottages behind the church for the first five years and then moved to our present place when we'd saved enough for a deposit."

"Nice houses where you are. Good size gardens too. I feel quite envious."

"Yes, and it's because of the gardens we moved there. Veronica's always had green fingers so she's as happy as Larry. Mind you, she was none too happy this morning when we heard that one of our neighbours was broken into last Thursday."

Robert was shocked. "What! That's horrible especially in a lovely village like Pentrillick. Was much taken?"

"No, thankfully nothing at all. Fortunately the bloke who lives there came home at around half ten from a barbecue with friends in Penzance and found the burglar in his living room. He didn't catch him though because as soon as the burglar heard Elliot in the house he escaped through the same window as he had got in through. Fair shook Elliot up though."

"I bet it did. Do I know this Elliot person?"

"I doubt it. I've never had reason to speak to him but Veronica has. His name is Elliot Harris. He's not lived in the house long and rents it from a couple who are working overseas for three years." Bernie chuckled, "The damn man has a set of drums and from time to time he plays music on a CD or whatever and drums along with it. Veronica said, it's a pity the burglar was disturbed because he might have been after the drum kit."

Robert laughed. "She doesn't like drums then?"

"Well, I wouldn't say that. I mean a lot of music would be pretty bland without rhythm, wouldn't it?"

"It would and if I'm honest I rather like to hear drums. In fact I like all percussion instruments, so I probably wouldn't mind having your neighbour near me."

"Oh, but, I can assure you, Robert, you wouldn't like Elliot Harris's drumming. He's dreadful and can't keep time."

"Ouch, that's not good then."

"No; still we can but hope he improves but I think it'll take a miracle."

"So going back to the attempted robbery, was this Elliot chap able to give the police a description of the would-be burglar?"

"I believe so but I don't know what it is. No doubt we'll find out if he strikes again. As I say, we didn't know anything about it until this morning when Veronica bumped into Tess along the main street."

Robert rested his arm on the side of the boat. "That's interesting what you've just told me because if the attempted burglary took place on Thursday night then it would have been the same night that young plumber lad was murdered, wouldn't it?"

Bernie took his hand off the rudder, removed his jacket and sat down. "You've got a point there, Robert. I wonder if there's a connection."

Shortly after ten o'clock on Sunday evening, Hetty and Lottie, wearing dark clothing, woolly hats - despite the warm evening - and soft soled shoes, left Primrose Cottage and walked down Long Lane into the village. At the bottom of the road they turned left and headed towards the church hoping they would see no-one they knew. The night was clear and dry;

29

the sky was scattered with twinkling stars but neither sister noticed for their heads were bent and their eyes were firmly fixed on the pavement. When they reached the church lichgate, Lottie sat down on the new bench in the street and nervously kept watch while Hetty slipped into the churchyard to retrieve the wilted plants. When a car drove by, Lottie lowered her head so that her face could not be seen and prayed that it would not park nearby. To her relief it continued on through the village and then disappeared round a bend.

It seemed much longer, but in less than three minutes Hetty was back on the pavement with the plants hidden inside a carrier bag along with some of the compost. Eager to get away, the sisters checked that no-one was around and then scuttled off along the road at a pace they were not used to. It wasn't until they were safely back in Long Lane and away from the street lights that they stopped to get their breath back and relax their leg muscles.

"I didn't bring the bit of ivy," puffed Hetty, "because we don't want that in our garden, do we? Although it was variegated and not the wild stuff."

Lottie was saddened. "Did you just leave it there on its own amongst the dandelion seeds to die?"

"Yes and no. I left it but not on its own to die. I pushed its root first into a gap between the stones in the wall. And don't worry, I forced in a bit of compost too and watered it with rain water from the urn on Septimus Pentreath's grave."

"Who on earth is Septimus Pentreath?"

"I haven't the foggiest idea. All I know is he shuffled off his mortal coil in 1752."

The following morning, as soon as it was light, the sisters took the flowers into their back garden, and in case word got out that they had been taken from the churchyard, they planted them amongst the yellow and orange marigolds so they would not be spotted if their neighbours on either side should peep over the garden walls.

When the task was completed, Hetty stood back and brushed earth from her hands as her sister watered the rescued plants. "That's a good job done, Lottie. I think we should be proud of ourselves and I'm sure the little flowers really appreciate our efforts. In fact they look better already."

"I agree, saving them can be our good deed for the day but we must never ever tell anyone about it, Het, because I'm pretty sure that crossing the blue and white tape *is* a criminal offence and I don't fancy being collared by the police."

Chapter Six

Just before eleven on Monday morning, Kitty arrived at Primrose Cottage, and as Hetty put the kettle on to make tea, Debbie arrived.

"Not late, am I?" Debbie asked, as Lottie escorted her into the living room, "I would have been here earlier but some chap arrived doing a survey so I answered his questions because Gideon didn't want to as he needed to get ready for work."

"A survey, what about?" Lottie asked.

"Oh, the usual stuff. You know, what do we watch on the telly? Which newspapers do we read? Where do we do our main shopping? What are our hobbies? Which brand of toothpaste? And tedious stuff like that."

"How boring. I hope he doesn't come here." Hetty placed a tea tray on the table.

"What was he like?" Kitty asked.

Debbie wrinkled her nose. "Tallish, sandy coloured hair and blue eyes. He was ever so nice and had a lovely smile."

"Around thirtyish?" Kitty asked.

"Yes, I would say so."

"Sounds like the same chap that called on Tommy and me just before the wedding."

"Oh yes, come to think of it I remember you telling us that now."

Lottie pulled out a dining chair and sat down. "You mentioning newspapers, Debbie, has just reminded me that Bill has a reporter from the local rag coming to see him today for a story about his hanging basket. I think its association with the murder has rather captured everyone's imagination."

Kitty tutted. "Poor Bill. I hear that basket was his pride and joy and his one and only contribution for the competition. Still, I suppose there's plenty of time for him to do another one before the judging. Well, five weeks or so, that should be enough."

"I agree, and let's just hope that if he does do another it's a little more spectacular than the last one, because even I, as a doting mother have to admit that it was a little lacklustre but of course I was too much of a coward to tell him so."

"You're right there, Lottie, and we must keep our fingers crossed. Sandra's tubs and window boxes look amazing and it'd be a shame if Bill's efforts let the side down." Hetty chuckled as she poured the tea and Kitty and Debbie sat down at the table.

"Did I dream it or did you tell me that when Bill planted up the original basket he told Sandra that one day it would be the talk of the village?" Kitty asked.

Hetty nodded. "Yes he did and so in that respect he was spot on."

Debbie took a sip of tea. "But not quite for the reason he anticipated. Bless him."

"Oh, poor Bill," Lottie glanced across the room to where a photograph of Bill on his first day at school graced the sideboard.

"Is that a lemon drizzle?" Kitty pointed to the cake on the table, "Because it smells delicious."

Hetty stood up to cut the cake into slices. "It is. We got the recipe from Veronica who had made a couple for the coffee morning last Saturday. Everyone was raving about it." Hetty handed a piece to each of the ladies who expressed their thanks.

"Right, now we're all seated and being fed it's time we made a start at solving the latest crime," said Debbie, "So may I ask if anyone has had any bright ideas as to who might have bumped off poor Gavin Snow?" All shook their heads. "Damn, because neither have I and Gideon's not exactly been an inspiration."

Lottie bent down and picked up a faded flower which had fallen on the floor from a gloxinia plant on the window sill. "It's a bit odd this murder, isn't it? I mean, none of us actually knew Gavin Snow. In fact we don't know anything about him. I'm not even sure whether I ever saw him but I suppose I must have at some time or other."

"Well, let's make a list of what we do know and then we'll take it from there." Hetty picked up the pen she had placed on the table earlier and then opened a notebook.

To enable her to concentrate, Debbie closed her eyes. "The deceased's name was Gavin Snow. He worked for a construction firm and I believe it said on the local news that he was thirty nine years old. That's all I can contribute."

Hetty wrote that down. "Well, that's a start. Does anyone know if he was married?"

The other three ladies shook their heads.

"I wonder where the building firm doing the pub work is based," said Lottie, "I mean, are they from around here do you think?"

"Good point," Hetty cast a glance at the ladies around the table, "Does anyone know the answer to that?"

"I think they're from Cornwall but up the other end somewhere," stated Kitty, "If they were from round here they'd not be staying in the caravans, would they?"

"No, of course not. Silly me," Lottie caught crumbs in her hand as she took a bite of cake.

"I heard they're from Plymouth," said Debbie, "but we can't check it out because I've no idea what the firm is called."

"I suppose it must be written on the side of their vans," reasoned Lottie, "but I can't say that I've ever noticed despite having seen them several times over the past few months. All I know is that they're white."

"Good point," Hetty wrote down 'check out vans'. "It might give a website address too then we can Google them."

"We can Google them without knowing the website as long as we have the name and location." Lottie finished her slice of cake and wondered if it would be greedy to have a second.

"True, true. So, can anyone else add anything?" Hetty asked, "Anything at all because this page looks very bare."

"He was tall and skinny with bushy eyebrows and he had a small straggly beard. His hair was long and he tied it back in a ponytail. A bit hippyish looking in fact," babbled Debbie.

Kitty nodded her head. "I thought that when I saw him outside the hotel one evening when Tommy and I were walking the dog. His legs were so skinny they didn't look strong enough to hold him up."

"Oh, is that right?" Lottie said, "I know who you mean now then. Such a shame as he was a nice looking lad and he had a smiley face."

Hetty laid down her pen. "I'm not sure that a description of him helps at all, especially the size and strength of his legs."

"No, I suppose it doesn't," agreed Debbie, "but that's all I can think of."

Hetty picked up her pen again. "Okay, so let's move on. Does anyone know of anyone who might have spoken to him at all? Other than his work mates that is. After all they've been here for several months now so they must have mingled a bit with the locals."

"I don't think Gideon has," reflected Debbie, "because their paths would have been unlikely to cross."

"Nor Tommy," said Kitty, "although he knew who Gavin was when we saw him outside the hotel because he told me and that's how I knew he had skinny legs."

Lottie's face lit up. "Sid has. I remember Zac saying not long ago that Sid had joined the tradesmen on several occasions when they've all been in the hotel bar for a drink at the same time."

"Yes, of course. Thank heavens, we're getting somewhere at last." Hetty wrote down on the page in capital letters, INTEROGATE SID.

Chapter Seven

Inside the office at Pentrillick House, Emma, the events manager, sat with Tristan and Samantha Liddicott-Treen discussing the Pentrillick in Bloom competition.

"I've was thinking this morning while in the shower that because the interest is so high and we've been swamped with entry forms it might be worth adding another prize to the competition for an overall winner," Tristan announced. "What do you think?"

"Yes, that's a good idea," agreed Emma, "I'm sure the more prizes there are the more effort people will make. Having said that the village is looking really lovely already and the scent along the main street in the evening is quite breath-taking."

Samantha agreed. "Yes, that's a really nice idea and I assume you're meaning something along the lines of Best in Show like they have at Chelsea."

"That's precisely what I mean but of course we can't call it Best in Show because it's not a show."

Emma picked up her pen to make notes. "What shall we call it then?"

"I don't know," Tristan looked at his wife, "any suggestions, Sam?"

Samantha shook her head.

Emma tapped the pen against her teeth. "You'll probably think it's a bit daft but how about the Green Fingers Award?"

Samantha's face lit up. "Or cup."

Emma clapped her hands. "Yes, cup, that's much better."

Tristan nodded. "I agree and so The Green Fingers Cup it shall be and we'll get one done specially. Now, Emma, if you can print off details stating that there is to be an extra prize, we'll get the addendum placed next to the original posters and also get it mentioned in the July edition of the Pentrillick Gazette, if it's not already too late."

Emma glanced at the calendar. "I think we'll just manage to scrape in as I believe they go to print on the penultimate day of each month."

"Excellent."

"While we're on the subject, who's going to judge the competition?" Samantha asked. "I mean, it can't be anyone from around here as it would be unfair and there really needs to be more than one judge anyway to get a balanced view."

"I had thought of that and I've several people in mind who I might invite down to spend the weekend with us and do the judging while they're here. Anyway, leave that with me, my love. I'll make sure that whoever it is, is a fair minded person with diverse horticultural knowledge."

"Has your dad got his hanging basket back yet?" Lottie asked Zac who had called at Primrose Cottage with Hetty's sunhat left at the Old Bakehouse by his great aunt during her last visit.

Zac shook his head. "No: forensics still have it and Sid reckons they'll probably hang on to it as it might be exhibit A or something like that."

Hetty tutted. "That's if they ever catch who did it and it goes to court. At the moment nothing seems to be happening and I haven't even heard of any suspects being questioned. Having said that I should imagine whoever did it isn't from around here anyway but fear not, Zac, we shall do our best to sniff out the no-good and see him brought to justice."

"Hmm, Dad said you'd most likely be having a go."

Lottie's lips quivered. "Oh dear. I hate the idea of Bill's hanging basket being a murder weapon."

"Yeah, poor Dad, he's not taken it very well. The girls and me used to ridicule his old basket and now we feel really mean."

"Oh, well, I suppose he'll sulk for a while but he'll soon get over it. He always took things to heart when he was little, didn't he, Lottie?"

"He did and I think we ought to buy him a replacement to cheer him up as it's unlikely he'll get his original one back this summer or maybe not even this year and he'll need one for the competition. He can't leave an empty bracket on the wall."

Zac sat down on the arm of the sofa. "No need for you to buy him a basket because Mum's going shopping today and she's intending to get him a couple and another bracket so that he can put one on either side of the door. I think in a way she's quite pleased. Not about Gavin Snow, of course, but she's pleased the basket's gone because she said it was off balance only having one and the chances of it ever looking fantastic were very, very slim."

Lottie nodded. "Yes, sadly I have to agree."

"Do you know if the police tape has gone from the churchyard yet?" Talk of Bill's hanging basket pricked Hetty's conscience.

"Funny you should ask that because Sid was only saying yesterday that two coppers were in the churchyard doing just that when he walked by and he heard one of them say someone had taken away Dad's plants. Sid asked me if it was Dad and I said no because Dad would never have dared cross the blue and white tape, he's much too law abiding for that. I hope the coppers don't think it was him though."

"I'm sure they wouldn't. As you say your dad is as honest as the day is long." Lottie felt the colour rise in her cheeks.

"That's what Mum said. He didn't take them though so he has nothing to fear." Zac stood up, "Anyway, I better get off now or I'll be late for work and have Sid on the warpath. See you whenever."

"Yes, off you go." Hetty blew him a kiss.

Lottie hugged her grandson and then escorted him to the front door.

After Zac had gone, Hetty and Lottie took Albert, Hetty's Yorkshire terrier, for a walk down Long Lane towards the village. At the bottom of the hill, they dawdled past the Crown and Anchor determined to take in as much as they could of the building work without looking too nosy. In the newly acquired field, stood the four caravans providing temporary housing for the builders; the end nearest the pub had been dug out and filled with hard-core prior to being tarmacked for the new car parking area.

Lottie waved her hand towards the caravans. "I was going to say that the tradesmen will each have a caravan to himself now there are only four of them left on site but of course there are only three now that poor old Gavin's gone and as we know they're not sending down another plumber because Sid and Zac are finishing the work instead."

"I suppose it could be said that it's an ill wind and so forth. I mean Gavin having gone and his work being passed on to Sid and Zac. Although I heard that Gavin's work is nearly all done, so were he still here he'd be off soon anyway."

"Yes, you're right. Just the radiators to be fitted in the new letting rooms. But Sid and Zac didn't need the extra work anyway. They've already got quite enough on their plates with the new houses being built."

"Yes, I suppose so."

"Talking of the new houses, shall we go up the lane and see how they're coming on, Het? I reckon they'll be done soon."

Hetty nodded with enthusiasm. "Yes, good idea. The last time we went up that way they'd only just dug out the footings and we couldn't visualise how it's going to look."

The construction of the new housing estate was commissioned by a local housing association and lay up a narrow lane in a field behind a care home for the elderly. In all there were to be twenty new homes. Six for purchase on the open market, four part-ownership, part-rent and ten for rent by local people with connections to Pentrillick.

"The houses would have nice sea views were it not for the care home," observed Hetty as the stopped by the site entrance, "It's a pity they didn't get a field further up the hill but then I suppose that would have meant taking water and other amenities up there which would add to the cost."

"The ones at the front here by the lane won't have a sea view, Het, but those furthest away will and no doubt they'll be the ones that are to be sold on the open market."

"Yes, I should imagine you're right. Anyway, it's a nice spot but would you like to live up here?" Hetty pulled back Albert who seeing men at work wanted to visit them.

Lottie shook her head. "I don't think so. I mean, I would if we didn't have our place but I wouldn't want to swap even though it would be nice to have everything brand new and be able to start a garden from scratch."

"I think I agree and we know and like our neighbours too. There's a lot to be said for that."

As there was very little to be seen from the site entrance the sisters turned and walked back down the lane. Just before they reached the bottom they met Kitty's husband walking his dog.

"Good morning, ladies." Tommy tipped his cap, "Have you been to take a look at the new development?"

"We have," said Lottie, "not that there's much to see without going on site."

Tommy looked over his shoulder. "Don't tell anyone, especially Kitty, but I often take a quick walk round the site when I walk the dog up here in the evening. It fascinates me. I wish I'd been involved in the building trade. It must be nice to look at houses and say I helped build that."

Hetty smiled. "Mum's the word but you've sowed seeds in my mind now and we might do the same before too long. Although with a murderer in our midst it doesn't really pay to go far off the beaten track, especially somewhere like this where as yet there are no streetlights."

"And don't forget there's also a burglar," said Tommy, "although he's probably not a violent man."

"Having nearly got caught he probably won't try again," reasoned Lottie, "after all it must have put the wind up him when the householder came home."

"Ah, but there's been another since then. One of the farms so I heard but I don't know which one yet."

Hetty gasped. "When was that? Was anything taken?"

"Yes, something was taken but I don't know what or when it happened. No doubt we'll find out in due course."

After bingo on Tuesday evening, where they had briefly discussed the latest burglary, Hetty, Lottie and Debbie walked along the main street to the Pentrillick Hotel for a glass or two of wine and to put the world to rights. They sat at their usual table by the window and after buying drinks subtly glanced at the other tables to see if there was anyone in that they knew. To their surprise, Clara Bragg, the cook at the care home was sitting at a corner table opposite a man who was unknown to them.

"Hmm, I wonder who he is." Hetty tried to recollect whether or not she had seen him before.

"Nice looking chap, whoever he might be," Debbie took a June copy of the Pentrillick Gazette from the window sill and pretended to read it so that she was able to peep over its top.

"I suppose he must be her chap," reasoned Lottie, "He's certainly not her husband because we know through Sandra that she's not married."

Hetty turned her head to get a better look at the couple. "I can't see any resemblance but perhaps he's her brother, cousin or something like that or he might even be someone she's meeting for the first time through a dating agency. To be honest, the list is endless."

"He might even be her penfriend and they're meeting up after writing to each other for years since they were children." Debbie flicked through the pages of the Gazette and then returned it to the window sill.

"Do people still have penfriends?" Hetty asked, "I mean surely with all the technology and stuff today something like that would be dead old hat."

"Yes, I suppose that might be the case, but the reason I suggested that is because there's a pen and some sheets of paper on the table between them so it could be a letter that one of them sent."

"Is there?" Hetty deliberately knocked her handbag onto the floor so that she could get a better look while retrieving it. "You're right, Debbie. In which case I reckon he's a journalist."

"Really! But if that's the case, what might be she telling him, Het?"

"I don't know, but journalists like a good story so she's probably got some information about Gavin's death."

Debbie gasped. "In which case she should go to the police. It's against the law to withhold information."

43

"No," laughed Lottie, "I think it's more likely she's telling him how she's going to win the Pentrillick in Bloom competition. In fact I bet he's the gardening correspondent of a local newspaper and she's charming him to make sure that there's a big article about her when she scoops first prize."

"Humph! If she does," scoffed Hetty.

Chapter Eight

On Wednesday morning after the girls had gone to school and Zac had gone to work, Sandra told Bill who had the day off from the supermarket where he worked, that she was going to the garden centre for a bag of compost and asked if he wanted to go with her.

"Why do you need more compost? Surely you've done enough pots and so forth already."

"Yes, but the compost has bedded down a lot in some of them and so I want to top them up. I also need to pot up some of the fuchsia cuttings I took a few weeks back."

"Oh, I see." Bill seemed hesitant.

"So are you coming or not? Because I'd like to go soon as I have to be at work at three this afternoon."

Bill stood up. "Yes, I might as well and then I can use some of your compost to fill the new baskets you bought for me. We'll go in my car though because I need to pop into the garage to see if they've a tyre to fit and I was going to do that today anyway."

Sandra took her mobile phone from a shelf and dropped it into her handbag. "Good, well, I'll just lock the back door then I'll be ready to go."

"Okay, I'll just change my shoes then I'll be ready too."

"So have you any idea what you're going to put in your baskets this time?" Sandra asked as they left the house and walked around the corner into Goose Lane where Bill's car was parked.

"No, but I'll select something nice and showy from work. Got to support the firm you know."

Sandra groaned. She would rather he supported the garden centre so that she could have a say in what he bought but thought it best not to interfere.

The garden centre car park was nearly full; they parked beside a selection of huge potted palms then collected a trolley from the bay and placed a large bag of compost in the bottom.

"As it's such a lovely day, let's take a walk around the site." Sandra hoped by doing so something spectacular might catch Bill's eye.

"Okay and then we can pop in the coffee shop because someone at work told me they have fantastic blueberry muffins here and I didn't have much breakfast."

Sandra chatted as they hurriedly passed a section of shrubs and trees; but as she led Bill towards the area where bedding plants and colourful perennials were housed, she slowed the pace, yet despite her hints about flowers that would look wonderful in hanging baskets and compliment her tubs and window boxes, Bill's response lacked enthusiasm.

"Yes, they're all very pretty, Sandra, but I know I'll find the perfect plants at work and look forward to choosing something in my lunch hour."

"Okay, have it your way but don't ever say I didn't offer to help."

"I wouldn't dream of it."

After they'd consumed coffee and blueberry muffins, they went to the car. Bill put the compost into the boot and pushed the trolley back to its bay. As he returned to the car and sat down in the driver's seat, Sandra grabbed his arm. "Quick, duck."

"What?"

"Duck."

They both crouched down below the dashboard.

"What's the matter, Sandra? Why are we hiding?"

Sandra slowly lifted her head and looked towards cars parked a few rows back behind Bill's. "Look over there," she whispered, "that's Clara Bragg, the cook at the care home I was telling you about. You know, the one who boasts about her gardening skills and reckons she's going to win the first prize."

Bill looked in the direction of Sandra's nodding head to where into the back of an estate car, Clara Bragg was carefully placing four professionally created hanging baskets each one dripping with flowers.

"The cheat," gasped Bill, "That's not allowed. Quick take a picture on your phone, Sandra."

Sandra leaned out of the window and took a picture just in time before Clara closed the car door and with a smug grin on her face pushed her empty trolley back across the car park.

On Wednesday morning, Sophie Shepherd locked the front door of Sea View Cottage and walked out towards her car. Ivor was already at work and she was due to begin her day at the dental surgery within the hour but en route she needed to get more petrol. As she unlocked the car door she thought she heard someone crying. Turning to look along the street she saw a woman sitting on the new bench at the bus stop, sobbing into her cupped hands. Wondering if the woman was hurt and needed help, Sophie crossed the road to ask.

The weeping woman seemed oblivious to Sophie's presence as she approached and so she knelt down in front of her and spoke softly, "Hi, my name's Sophie. Are you alright? Is there anything I can do to help?"

The woman stopped crying, pulled a tissue from her sleeve and wiped her eyes. "Sorry, Sophie, I'm fine, really I am." She turned and pointed to the churchyard wall, "It's just...it's just that in there must be where poor Gavin was killed and as much as I want to, I can't bring myself to go in."

Sophie stood and then sat down beside the woman. "I take it you knew Gavin then?"

"Yes, yes, I knew him." Her soft voice was barely audible.

"Oh, I'm so sorry. It must have been a terrible shock for you. Were you very close?"

She nodded her head. "He's my husband or should I say he was." The tears again welled in her eyes. "I can't get my head round it. I mean, who can have done such a thing and why? He was so gentle, so peace loving and I'm sure he didn't have an enemy in the world, "she pushed her fringe from her eyes, "Although I suppose he must have had or he'd still be alive, wouldn't he?"

"Yes, and let's hope the police catch whoever it was soon. Not that it will bring your poor husband back." Sophie stood up, "Look, I'm really sorry but I have to go or I'll be late for work. Can I drop you anywhere on my way? I don't think you should be alone."

"No, thank you. I'm staying at the hotel and so don't have far to go. Anyway, I'd like to sit a little longer yet. I might even pluck up the courage to go into the churchyard," she smiled sweetly, "Thank you for your concern though. I really do appreciate it. I don't know anyone here, you see. I don't even know the chaps he works with. Worked with, I mean. They're just names I've heard him mention over the years."

Sophie squeezed the young widow's hands. "Well, if you ever need a shoulder to cry on please don't hesitate to call on us. My husband and I live over the road there in Sea View Cottage and you'd be most welcome anytime. Anytime at all."

"Thank you, I'll bear that in mind, Sophie."

Inside Primrose Cottage, Lottie stood on a dining chair cleaning the sitting room windows and singing along with an old sixties song on the radio.

Hetty was in the kitchen washing the breakfast dishes; as she placed a dish on the draining board she heard her sister scream. With soap suds on her hands, she dashed down the hallway to see what was wrong. Lottie was still on the chair but her face was devoid of colour.

"What's the matter? Are you ill? Have you seen a spider?" Hetty helped her sister down from the chair.

"No, no spider and I'm not ill, but look outside." Lottie nodded towards the window.

Hetty's scream was little more than a squeak. "Police. Oh my God, Lottie. They must know about the plants."

The sisters watched in horror as two police officers stepped from their car and walked through the garden gates.

"What shall we do, Het?" Lottie's hands were shaking, "Shall we hide and pretend we're not here?"

Hetty switched off the radio. "No because they probably saw you at the window. We must act calm and deny knowing anything about the whereabouts of the plants."

"But what if we were seen on Sunday night?"

"I'm sure we weren't. No cars went by when we were at the church."

"One did," said Lottie, "but I kept my head bowed and it didn't stop so it was probably just passing through."

The doorbell rang. Lottie placed a hand over her mouth to muffle her scream while Hetty wiped her damp hands on the front of her cardigan and cautiously opened the door. She smiled as sweetly as her fear would allow.

"Good morning, officers and what can I do for you?"

The police officers produced identification and recited their names; the senior of the two was a tall, slim man no more than forty years of age and his female companion was petite and looked to be in her twenties. Both had friendly smiles.

"Good morning, ma'am," said the male officer, "As you probably know there has been one burglary and one attempted burglary in the village in recent weeks and we're doing house to house enquiries to see if residents have noticed any suspicious characters hanging around their property."

Hetty bit her lip. She felt like crying. "Oh, that's wonderful, wonderful. Thank goodness for that. I mean, yes we had heard about the burglaries. Shocking isn't it? I can't say that I've seen any suspicious people around though. Have you, Lottie?" Hetty felt her face flush. She knew she was babbling.

Lottie who had joined her sister in the doorway was unable to wipe the huge grin from her face. "No, I've not seen anyone hanging around. Have you any idea what the person in question looks like, officer? It might help if we knew who we're looking for."

"True, true," Hetty added, "I mean are we looking for a man or a woman. Although I suppose it has to be a man because I doubt that many burglars are women. Or perhaps they are. It's not something I've ever given much thought to."

"Err, yes." The officer looked bemused as he glanced at his colleague and then at his notes. "According to the gentleman who disturbed the burglar in the first case, he was a white man in his mid-thirties, around five ten in height and medium build and on the back of his hand he has a tattoo. He also has thick, dark brown, curly hair and a droopy moustache."

"Wonderful. He sounds like Jason King, doesn't he, Lottie?" Hetty's relief had made her feel frivolous.

The female police officer's face lit up. "Do you mean to say you know him?"

"No, no, no, he's not real, you see. Jason King was a television character played by Peter Wyngarde. If I remember correctly the programme was called Jason King."

Lottie nodded. "That's right and another was called Department S. Something like that anyway."

"But whatever, it was in the very early nineteen seventies. Which I daresay was before you were even born."

Lottie nodded. "Oh yes, long before you were born, dear. In fact long before either of you were born."

Both police officers were clearly disappointed.

"Oh, I see. Well if you do see anyone looking like your err Jason King perhaps you'll get in touch." The male officer closed his note book.

"Yes, of course, we'll keep our eyes open from now on, won't we, Lottie?"

"Yes, it'll be fun."

"Well, um, thank you, we appreciate that and should you see him, please ring this number." The officer handed Hetty a card.

"Would you like a cup of tea?" Lottie wanted to hug the officers but thought tea would be a more acceptable option.

"That's very kind but no thank you. We need to get on and try and track this man down before he strikes again."

"Yes, of course. Thank you for calling."

Hetty closed the door and then dashed into the living room with Lottie where they watched the officers drive away. "Phew, that was close."

Lottie sat down before her legs gave way. "I shall never, ever, break the law again."

Chapter Nine

Sid woke up early on Saturday morning and looked out of the window of his home in Honeysuckle Drive. Pleased that the weather was looking good for the weekend and his time off work he pondered over whether to have a game of golf or potter around in the garden instead. And then there was the gardening competition to think about. Was he going to enter it or not? His garden was looking good and he had the entry form but as yet had not filled it in and the last date for entry was fast approaching. As he put two thick slices of bread in the toaster, his mobile phone rang.

"Oh, hello, Hetty, what can I do for you?"

Hetty explained how she Lottie, Debbie and Kitty were trying to get to the bottom of Gavin Snow's untimely demise and wondered if he, having met with Gavin, could give them an insight into his character. Sid was amused. He knew what the ladies were like but they were harmless enough.

"I can't tell you much," said Sid, "but I did chat with him a few times and his workmates too. If you and your accomplices care to call round sometime today I'll put you in the picture and in return you can all give me some advice on whether or not I should enter the Pentrillick in Bloom competition."

"Oh, thank you, Sid, you're a star and we really do appreciate it. Debbie and Kitty are out this morning with their respective husbands but Lottie and I will be with you at eleven on the dot."

After their meeting with Sid, Hetty and Lottie walked down to the charity shop, for the previous afternoon Lottie had discovered a hole in her favourite blouse and knowing it would no longer be stocked by the store where she had bought it she wanted to see if the charity shop had anything similar. As they walked along the main street they were pleased to see several people out in their gardens and on the pavement tending tubs, pots, window boxes and hanging baskets.

Inside the charity shop they found Bernie the Boatman's wife, Veronica asking Maisie and Daisy the shop's volunteers if they would be interested in joining a gardening club for which she had a poster to put in the shop window. Both ladies were very enthusiastic and relayed the idea to Lottie and Hetty as they stepped over the threshold.

Lottie looked at the poster. "You can count me in, Veronica, it sounds right up my street."

"And mine too," Hetty was equally enthusiastic.

"So, where and when would the meetings be held?" Lottie asked. "It doesn't say on the poster."

"That's because it's yet to be confirmed. We're hoping that Monday evenings will be okay and we're thinking about hiring the village hall. When Monday was first suggested I thought we'd be unlucky because I was sure it was the night the Pentrillick Players met but I've checked it out and it appears they've swapped to Wednesdays this year instead."

Hetty nodded. "Yes, they have because someone couldn't make Mondays but I can't remember who."

"I think it was Marlene," said Maisie.

"Yes, you're right it was," Lottie agreed. "As for starting a gardening club I think it's a brilliant idea and I'm really surprised that nobody has thought of it before. So well done, Veronica."

"Actually I can't take the credit because it wasn't my idea. It was suggested to me by Sally and Robert Oliver when they popped in for the coffee morning last week."

Hetty frowned. "Sally and Robert Oliver as in the newcomers who live above this shop?" Hetty looked at the ceiling.

"Yes, that's right."

"But they don't have a garden," Lottie was confused.

Veronica smiled. "No, but they're both very knowledgeable and had a lovely garden at their home in Birmingham before they moved to Cornwall. They've shown me pictures of it and it really is stunning."

"It must have been hard for them to leave it then," reasoned Hetty. "I was sorry to leave my garden when we moved down here but it could never have been described as stunning. Not by any stretch of the imagination."

"I said that to Sally when she showed me the pictures and she said the people who bought their house were keen gardeners too so they felt sure that it would be in good hands and not concreted over as some are inclined to do."

Daisy looked towards the door and gave a welcoming smile to a new customer as he entered the shop; she then returned her focus to the gardening conversation. "Anyway, they have house plants everywhere in the flat because we've seen them, and window boxes at the back because it's south facing so they do have a little greenery."

"But you can't see the window boxes unless you're down on the beach," added Maisie, "which is a shame."

"Yes, that is a pity," Lottie agreed, "because it means they won't be able to enter the Pentrillick in Bloom competition if they're on the back."

"No, but it was the competition that kindled the idea of a gardening club. They're very enthusiastic about it and see it as a way of making new friends who will of course be like-minded."

The afternoon was sunny and warm, and so after the sisters left the charity shop they agreed that rather than go home they would take a walk down to the beach and watch the sea for a while. When they arrived they popped into the beach shop for ice creams and then crossed the sand and shingle in search of an empty bench. They were in luck for a family were just in the throes of leaving. Once seated, the ladies kicked off their sandals and made themselves comfortable.

"Is that a newspaper tucked in your end of the bench, Het?" Lottie asked as she placed a carrier bag containing her new blouse by her feet.

Hetty pulled at the paper. "Yes, do you want it? It looks clean and so hasn't been here long."

"Depends what it is because it's just occurred to me that we've not seen the local paper yet and there might be something in it about Bill's hanging basket."

Hetty picked up the newspaper and tried to unfold it with one hand. It was not possible. "Hold my ice cream please."

Lottie took the cornet and watched as her sister unfolded the paper. Hetty looked at the date. "Yes, it's our local and it is this week's. There's nothing on the front page though."

She passed the paper to Lottie who placed it on her lap. "I must finish this first as it's melting rapidly."

Once both ice creams were eaten, Lottie opened up the newspaper and thumbed through the pages. There was nothing until she reached the centre where a two page spread was headed *Death by Hanging Basket.* She scanned the article and then passed the paper to Hetty. "Poor Bill. Why did it have to happen to him?"

Hetty read the first few paragraphs and then gave up. Most of what was written about Gavin's death she already knew and the rest appeared to be about the Pentrillick in Bloom competition. "I don't know, Lottie, but what with the murder and the burglaries I'm beginning to think Pentrillick isn't a very nice place to live in."

"Oh, don't say that, Het. I mean, the chances are that Gavin's death is nothing to do with anyone here and I daresay the burglar lives elsewhere too."

"I suppose you're right. Anyway, we mustn't grumble about it because trying to fathom out why Gavin was killed and who did it as well as keeping a look out for a Jason King burglar lookalike is enough to keep us busy for the time being and probably the whole summer as well."

Lottie leaned forwards on the bench. "Talking of Jason King lookalikes. Look over there, Het."

Hetty looked in the direction where her sister subtly pointed. Sitting on a blanket not far from the water's edge was someone with a head of thick, curly dark brown hair. He wore jeans and a white T shirt and leaned back on his tanned arms; judging by the angle of his head it seemed he was watching bathers in the sea.

"Shall we go for a little stroll along the beach?" Hetty asked, "We need to see whether or not he has a droopy moustache."

"Yes, but to do that we'll have to walk in front of him so I suggest, that so we don't look out of place, we paddle along the shoreline."

"Excellent idea," Hetty excitedly rolled up her trouser legs and then picked up her sandals. Lottie tucked the newspaper in the bag containing her new blouse and then did likewise.

The sand and shingle struck warm to their feet as they made their way down the beach towards the sea; it was in sharp contrast to the water's temperature as they stepped into the falling waves.

Chatting and laughing they made their way along the shore jumping in and out of the waves like children. At the same time they made a point of not looking in the direction of their suspect until they were almost in his line of vision. When they knew they were in the ideal position to see his face, both linked arms, glanced across the beach and pointed to the backs of buildings on pretence of looking at the pub's new extension. They then lowered their heads and subtly glanced at the Jason King lookalike. He was not looking in their direction but they could clearly see his face and to their disappointment, they saw their suspect was clean shaven, wore make-up and was clearly a woman.

Chapter Ten

On Sunday morning, Hetty and Lottie went to church where once again the service was taken by the vicar from a neighbouring parish.

"When are Sam and Martha due back?" Lottie asked Kitty, as she joined them in the churchyard, "They've been gone for two weeks now."

Kitty removed her lightweight jacket for it was considerably warmer out in the sun than in the church where she had played the organ. "Not for another week or so. They're back from Italy but are currently up-country visiting friends and relatives who were unable to make the wedding and then they're going to spend a few days with Sam's parents. Vicar George is more than happy to cover for him, in fact only this morning he was saying he'll miss us all and has really enjoyed his involvement with the village."

Hetty tutted. "Well, he's certainly been kept on his toes and I'm sure when he agreed to take over Sam's duties he never envisaged a murder in the churchyard."

Lottie glanced towards the porch where the vicar was talking to one of the parishioners. "No and I hope it never happens to him again although he seems to have coped very well."

"We saw your Tommy the other day and he said there had been another burglary," said Hetty, "And since then we've had the police round doing house to house enquiries and so forth. Have you heard any more?"

Kitty folded her jacket and placed it inside her voluminous handbag. "Only that it was a farm a mile or so outside the village. It's called Willow Farm and is owned and run by the Glover family. I believe they were out for a meal that evening celebrating their son's twenty first. I've seen the family around but never actually met any of them. Jimmy and Tamsin Glover are teetotallers I believe and so they never come to the pub. I can't really tell you any more than that."

Hetty looked relieved. "Well with any luck whoever the burglar is he's targeting places elsewhere now."

"And hopefully," said Lottie, "he'll slip up soon and get caught."

Kitty's husband, Tommy who had been chatting to one of the church wardens had heard what was said. "I've just learned a bit more. Apparently the Glovers lost a substantial amount of cash taken in the robbery which they kept in the drawer of a dresser. It's not known how much but it was money they were saving for their son's wedding."

Lottie tutted. "That's horrid. Poor people."

"I'm surprised that anyone still saves cash," said Hetty, "Apart from my collection at church and a few pounds here and there for when I buy something in the charity shop, I pay for everything else with my debit card."

"I suppose the money was from cash sales, you know farmers' markets and things like that," reasoned Kitty, "And as for using debit and credit cards, I think it's a shame that cash is used so little nowadays because at least when you hand over real money it gives you a better idea of how much you've actually spent, if you see what I mean."

Lottie nodded her head vigorously. "Absolutely, I wholeheartedly agree with you there, Kitty but perhaps it's just an age thing or maybe we're Luddites."

"Tomato plants," gasped Sandra, on Sunday afternoon as Bill returned home from work with a cardboard box containing six small pots. She watched in disbelief as he placed the box on the dining room table and then closed the front door.

"Yes, I think they will wow the judges, don't you?"

Sandra sat down. "No, I don't. If the weather is poor they could well get blight and their leaves are likely to discolour whatever when in the confines of a hanging basket. They also like lots of sun and might get battered by the wind."

"Same with flowers and on the front of the house they will get a lot of sun providing it's shining of course. Anyway they're recommended for hanging baskets and unlike flowers we'll be able to eat the fruit. Seems a win-win situation to me." Bill took the label from one of the pots and passed it to his wife. "Take a peek at this, Sandra, and see how fantastic they're going to look."

"Oh, Bill, things never look as good in reality as they do on pictures and in books, you should know that."

"Well, these will. I've bought tomato plant food and I looked up how to care for them in my lunch break. And like you, I shall be joining the new gardening club."

"You will? That's wonderful." Sandra felt a ray of hope and prayed that someone there might have more influence than she appeared to have.

"Yes, I am and you'll see, Sandra my hanging baskets are going to look stunning. What's more, the yellow flowers will match the front door beautifully."

"Yellow flowers," mumbled Sandra wistfully as she thought longingly of the yellow flowers in the original hanging basket.

"Right," Hetty pulled back a chair and sat down at the dining table in the sitting room of Primrose Cottage, "time to get down to the serious business of trying to find out who killed poor Gavin Snow. As you know, Lottie and I met up with Sid on Saturday morning and he gave us an insight as to what Gavin and his workmates are like."

"I hope you made notes," said Debbie, "because ladies of our age are likely to get things muddled and we don't want to end up accusing someone of wrong doing who is completely innocent."

"Accuse someone of wrong doing who is completely innocent," spluttered Hetty, "as if we would, Debbie. But fear not because we did make notes."

"Good, so who are you going to start with?" Kitty pushed back her chair so that she had room to cross her legs.

Hetty opened up her notepad. "I thought we'd start with Gavin Snow."

"Gavin, but he's the victim so why start with him?" Debbie was puzzled.

"To give us some idea of what he was like," Hetty cleared her throat, "Right, Gavin was thirty nine years old, he was born in Taunton and went to school there. After school he trained as a plumber and moved to Bodmin after he got married. His wife, or should I say widow, came from Bodmin, you see and there he joined the construction firm who are doing the pub work."

"That's interesting. So the pub's workmen come all the way from Bodmin," said Debbie.

"That's right, and Lottie and I reckon it's just short of fifty miles."

Kitty put up her hand as though at school. "So who did Gavin marry, Het? I mean, what line of work and so forth does she do?"

"And are there any children?" Debbie added.

Hetty looked at her notes. "No children. Her name is Miranda. Sid told us that it was love at first sight as far as

Gavin was concerned. Her maiden name was Frost, you see, and so the poor lad felt sure they were meant for each other."

"Oh, that's really sweet," cooed Debbie, "Frost and Snow. What a lovely combination."

At the thought of snow, Kitty shuddered. "Hmm, but not my favourite weather, not these days anyway."

"Nice to look at though," persisted Debbie, "and snow scenes make gorgeous Christmas cards." Hetty coughed. "Sorry, Hetty, please continue and perhaps you can tell us where she worked."

Hetty looked at her notes. "She works for a bank. I don't know which one or what she does but I don't think it matters anyway."

"No, I suppose not," agreed Debbie, "Anything else?"

"Well according to Sid, Gavin was a genial fella, easy going, caring, a keen golfer and very laid back. In fact Sid's exact words were that he wouldn't hurt a fly."

"Not the sort to have got into an argument then," reasoned Kitty.

Debbie frowned. "I wonder what made him go into the churchyard. I mean, we know he'd been to the hotel for a drink and was on his way back to his caravan, but why go into the churchyard in the first place?"

"Good point," Kitty agreed.

Hetty gasped. "Oh, my goodness, you don't think he went in there to meet someone, do you?"

"What, like a woman?" Lottie was aghast.

"Well, yes, I suppose that's what I mean."

"Surely not," tutted Kitty, "he was a married man and you just told us, Hetty that Gavin reckoned because of their surnames he and his wife were meant for each other."

"Yes, but that was when they first met. Things change and he was away from home."

Debbie leaned her elbows on the table. "But if he had gone there to meet someone, who could it be?"

Hetty's eyes flashed. "If I had to make a guess my money would be on Clara Bragg."

"Clara Bragg!" laughed Lottie, "Why on earth do you say that?"

"Well," Hetty paused for thought, "I suppose because she seems to pop up everywhere these days. You know, she was at Bernie and Veronica's coffee morning the other Saturday, she's joined the drama group, I've heard she might join the gardening club and she's even been to bingo a couple of times too."

"But we go to all of those things as well," reasoned Lottie.

"And she's never been to church," voiced Kitty.

Debbie shook her head. "I think we're going off the subject a bit. What's more, Gavin certainly did not meet Clara in the churchyard on the night he died because she was away on holiday in Greece that week and didn't get back until early evening the following day. I recall her saying it was very hot there."

"Yes, you're right," agreed Kitty, "I heard her going on about her suntan at Veronica and Bernie's coffee morning which of course was the day after she got back."

Hetty tapped her fingers on the table. "So out of curiosity, who did she go to Greece with? As far as I know she doesn't have a partner."

"She went on one of the package deals they do for singles," said Debbie, "something like that."

Kitty sighed. "Did she? That's really sad, poor Clara."

"Yes," agreed Debbie, "I'd not really thought about it but it must be horrible to have no partner and live alone."

Hetty laughed. "Well I've never married and for years I lived alone and can assure you it's not that bad. In fact, when I was working I rather liked it."

63

"Anyway, she might have a partner now," suggested Debbie, "Remember we saw her in the hotel the other day having a drink with a good-looking chap."

Hetty nodded. "Yes, but I thought we agreed that he was probably a gardening journalist."

Debbie tapped her nicely manicured nails on the table top. "True, but then on the other hand we might well be wrong and he could be as you suggested, Het, someone she was meeting for the first time through a dating agency."

"Well whatever, I think she's one to keep an eye on as we know she's moody and sulks a lot which means she's probably hot-headed too."

"She's moody and sulks a lot," gasped Lottie, "whatever makes you say that, Het?"

"Surely you've not forgotten how grumpy she was when she didn't get the part she wanted in the new play? She showed off rotten when they gave it to Marlene who is a much better actress anyway."

"But you don't like Marlene," laughed Kitty.

"And you didn't get the part you wanted either, Hetty Tonkins," Lottie reminded her, "So you'll be doing refreshments this year."

"Yes, but…"

Lottie wagged her finger at her sister. "No buts, Het, just get on with the character analysis. Discussing Clara's love life and her acting abilities has nothing whatsoever to do with Gavin's case."

Hetty's jaw dropped but she managed to suppress the urge to argue. She picked up her notepad. "Right, now the three chaps that Gavin worked with are Leo who does stone work age thirty eight, Max, likewise who is forty two and Vince a plasterer-cum-chippy who at fifty nine is looking forward to retirement. There were others, you know, brickies, roofers and so forth but they had already done their work and gone back to

Bodmin before Gavin died. Sid said they were all nice blokes and of the four left, now three, none of them struck him as aggressive although Max did get a bit argumentative one night after he'd been drinking shorts. It wasn't about anything serious though: Sid thinks it might even have been football."

"And talking of football, that's why Gavin was at the hotel drinking alone on the Thursday night that he died," divulged Lottie, "The other three were watching football on the telly in Vince's caravan and Gavin didn't want to watch it because according to Sid the only sport he liked was golf."

"I had wondered where the others were that night," said Kitty, "but forgot to mention it."

Debbie frowned. "So who's doing the electrics?"

"What?" Hetty put down her pen.

"The electrics at the pub."

"Oh, I see. It's Ian."

"What our local Ian?"

"Yes. Funny you should say that because I asked Sid the same question. Apparently one of the chaps the firm employs to do electrics is currently off sick because he fell off a ladder and the other is tied up with a job elsewhere so the firm's boss arranged for someone down here to do it and Ian got the job."

"Oh, I see," Debbie digested the information received. "There is another thing though that's just occurred to me and that is I wonder why the Dales gave the contract for the pub's work to a Bodmin company in the first place and not a firm down here."

Hetty turned over a page in the notepad. "Now that I do know. The firm's name, by the way is S. P. Roach & Son and apparently James and Ella had a pub in the Bodmin area before they came down here and the boss of the firm, Mr Roach, I assume, and some of his employees used to drink in their pub so when they bought the Crown and Anchor, James offered them the work. Probably because they felt they could trust them."

Debbie's eyebrows rose. "So James and Ella knew Gavin before he came down here to work."

"Good point," cried Lottie, "so they must be added to our list of suspects."

"Do we have one?" Kitty asked.

Hetty picked up and waved her notebook. "Oh yes, Kitty. Three of Gavin's work colleagues, and now the new licensees of the Crown and Anchor. Then there are newcomers Sally and Robert Oliver who live in the flat over the charity shop and the Shepherds at Sea View Cottage until we know more about them. Now all we need is a motive."

"The Shepherds at Sea View Cottage," laughed Kitty, "Don't be daft, Het. Ivor is a paramedic."

"So what. Harold Shipman was a doctor."

"But he…"

"I don't think you ought to include Ella either. She looks like she wouldn't say boo to a goose," laughed Debbie.

"You can't judge a book by its cover," insisted Hetty. "In fact it's just occurred to me that it might have been Ella that Gavin went to the churchyard to meet."

"Humph. That's even more bonkers than suggesting Clara Bragg," scoffed Lottie.

"Lottie's right," Kitty agreed. "Ella could never have murdered Gavin."

Hetty smirked. "I'm not saying that she did, because if I'm right and she met Gavin in the churchyard, then James would be the murderer having followed her there."

Ella Dale, oblivious of her good name being dragged through the mud, sat at her laptop in the office of the Crown and Anchor and selected bed linen for the new guest rooms. She had thought of carrying on the colour scheme of the old rooms which were in good decorative order but decided after a while that white bed linen might get monotonous and so instead opted for something completely different. The walls in each new room had already been painted a subtle shade of cream and matching carpets were due to be laid the following week so to compliment them she chose accessories in different colours for each room. For the first she chose yellow and the room rather than having a number would be known as the Buttercup Room. For the second she chose a light blue for the Forget-me-not Room. And finally she chose a pretty shade of mauve for the Lilac Room. Delighted with her choice she then ordered new beds, mattresses and bedside tables. There was no need for wardrobes as each room had one built in. Finally she ordered towels and bath mats to match the bedding.

"And the *piece de resistance* shall be my own paintings of the flowers specified for each room." Ella closed down her laptop, "A bit of painting will be the ideal project to keep me occupied between now and the grand opening."

Chapter Eleven

Just after Bill returned home from work there was a knock on the door of the Old Bakehouse.

"Norman," cried Bill, as he opened the door, "Good to see you, man. Come in, come in."

"Thanks, Bill." Norman wiped his feet on the doormat even though they were not dirty.

"I didn't expect to see you again so soon after the wedding." Bill closed the door.

"Well, that was only a flying visit, wasn't it? I mean, I had to get back to sort things out. I'm here for a week or so now though and as usual I'm staying at the hotel." He pointed to a shaft of sunlight shining through the dining room window: "the weather's looking good for a while too but then the sun always shines on the righteous."

"And the unrighteous," laughed Bill. He led Norman into the sitting room. "So when did you get here?"

"A couple of hours ago, so apart from a few familiar faces at the hotel you're the first person I've seen that I know."

Inside the sitting room, Sandra was cleaning the glass in the French doors. "Norman. I thought it sounded like your voice." She kissed his cheek, "Lovely to see you again."

The men sat down and Norman took several sheets of paper from his pocket. "If you're wondering why I'm here it's because when I was down for the wedding I heard about the new houses being built in the village and so when I got home I looked into them on-line and liked what I saw. Six are for sale apparently and I rather like the notion of buying one. I have a buyer for my place, you see. I didn't want to say anything at the wedding in case it fell through but it's looking pretty concrete now."

"Really, that's wonderful," said Sandra, "Zac and Sid are doing the plumbing on the new houses. Well, they were until the other day. They've taken a few days off to finish the plumbing work at the pub for the new licensees."

"I heard mention at the wedding that Alison and Ashley have gone from the pub. Such a shame as they were a really nice couple?"

Bill took the proffered sheets of paper from Norman's hands. "Yes, I have to agree. They're living in Penzance now. Alison's gone back to teaching and Ashley's writing a book."

Norman chuckled. "Rather him than me. I wouldn't know where to start."

"Me neither," Bill unfolded the sheets of paper.

"I suppose you've heard about the recent murder?" Sandra polished the last pane of glass and the stood back to check there were no smears.

"What!" Norman shook his head. "Good heavens, no, I haven't. Who was that then?"

"No-one you would know," Bill assured him, "He was one of the chaps working on the pub's refurbishment. His name was Gavin Snow."

"And he was a plumber," Sandra added, "that's why Zac and Sid are currently working at the pub. It's to finish the work poor Gavin started."

"His wife's here at the moment and she's staying at the hotel," said Bill, "I've not seen her but I'm told she's pretty, slim with short blonde hair and a gorgeous pair of legs."

"I see, well thanks for warning me. I'll be careful what I say to the poor lady if our paths cross as I should hate to put my foot in it."

Bill handed the house details to Sandra as she sat by his side on the sofa. "They look very impressive, Norman, although the pictures of the exterior are obviously computer generated. I think I should like to take a look at them for no other reason than curiosity."

"Then please come with me. I'd much rather have company than go on my own. It'd be nice to have a second opinion too because having inherited my place from Mum I've never actually bought a house before so the whole procedure is new to me."

The following day after he finished work, Bill met up with Norman and they went to visit the new housing estate. Sandra wished she could have gone with them but her work shift at the care home coincided with the time of Norman's appointment.

The builders had finished work for the day and so as prearranged the two men met up with someone from the agency handling the sale of the six houses. After donning hard hats and high visibility jackets they were shown the four of the remaining six houses for sale which were almost finished.

"What do you think?" Norman asked Bill, as they left the site and walked past the care home down the hill towards the main street.

"I liked them, especially the one on the corner. If I were in your position I wouldn't hesitate to go for that or any of the others for that matter. Having said that you probably wouldn't want the one on the corner because it has three bedrooms."

"Well, maybe I would. I might well have a lodger, you see."

"A lodger. Who?"

"Jackie."

"What Jackie as in your young next door neighbour?"

"Yes, I know she's keen to move down here and has been dropping lots of hints ever since I told her I had a buyer for my place. She really fell in love with Pentrillick when she was here last year and the people too."

"Well, that'll please my girls as she'll be able to teach them to play pool."

"That's just what Jackie's hoping to do."

On Tuesday night, after bingo, Hetty, Lottie and Debbie walked through the village towards the Pentrillick Hotel for a glass or two of wine.

"I'll be glad when the pub's open again," muttered Debbie. "The hotel is nice but it's too sterile, the lighting is too bright and just doesn't have the atmosphere that a pub does."

"It's a much longer walk as well," Hetty grumbled, "not that I mind walking if the weather's fine."

Debbie glanced back along the street. "No, I can't agree with you there, Het. I'd say the walk from the village hall to the hotel is about the same as the village hall to the pub."

"And so it is," agreed Hetty, "But it's a lot longer walking from the hotel to Blackberry Way than it is from the pub."

"Ah, yes of course. Silly me."

Feeling warm, Lottie unzipped her jacket. "Well, hopefully it won't be much longer 'til they open up. They were facing up the new extension block work with granite when Het and I walked past the other day and very nice it's looking too."

"And so are Bill's hanging baskets," Debbie looked up admiringly as they passed by the Old Bakehouse, "I thought he was bonkers putting in tomatoes but it seems a really good idea now and I should imagine no-one else will have done that so it might gain him and Sandra a few extra points."

"They should look good," laughed Lottie, "he tends them like babies and if the weather looks threatening he takes them indoors and hangs them in the utility room out the back."

"It's becoming an obsession," Hetty added. "He's determined to prove Sandra wrong and wants to show that he has green fingers."

"Talking of green fingers, they're starting to landscape the field and create the new pub gardens on Monday," Debbie revealed. "I know that because it's the gardeners from Pentrillick House who will be doing it and Gideon's one of the team and so is that new chap Robert who lives over the charity shop. Gideon sounded really enthusiastic when he was telling me about it."

"How exciting," gushed Lottie, "It'll be nice to have gardens to sit in on a summer's evening. The sun terrace as it was before the work began was lovely but it used to get very crowded during the holiday season. Having said that it will probably still be there and just the same after the alterations."

Hetty stepped off the kerb to avoid a lamppost. "It is still there and it looks no different. I saw it the other day when I took Albert for a run across the beach. In fact that part of the pub looks unchanged."

"Yes of course, I've seen it too," Lottie remembered glancing in that direction when they were on the beach attempting to establish the appearance of the Jason King lookalike.

On reaching the hotel they went inside and made a beeline for their usual table near to a window.

"Who's that over there knocking back gin and tonics?" Lottie nodded to a young blonde woman sitting at the bar.

"No idea," Debbie shuffled through her handbag to find her purse, "but I'd guess she's one of the hotel's guests. Why do you ask?"

"Well, I just wondered if she might be poor Gavin Snow's widow. The other day Bill was talking to that paramedic chappie who's living in Sea View Cottage and he told Bill that his wife had met Gavin's widow and that she's staying here at the hotel. I wondered if it might be her."

"What! She's in the village and staying here at the hotel? You didn't tell me that, Lottie Burton." Hetty was quite indignant and sat down heavily at the table.

"Sorry, Het. Must have slipped my mind. So what do you both think?" Lottie pulled out a chair and sat down.

The three ladies cast their eyes in the direction of the young woman sitting at the bar.

"She doesn't look much like a grieving widow," hissed Hetty.

Debbie nodded. "I have to agree. I certainly wouldn't be drinking like that if Gideon had just been murdered. God forbid."

"But the drink might be to deaden the pain," reasoned Lottie, "We all grieve in different ways."

"Yes, I suppose so," Debbie hung her bag on the back of her chair, "Anyway, your usual, ladies?"

"Yes please," Hetty and Lottie replied in unison.

While Debbie was at the bar, the sisters subtly watched the woman in question. She sat on a high stool, her right arm resting on the bar beside a small bottle of tonic water and in her left hand she held a tall tumbler. Her hair was blonde and bobbed, she wore pale blue shorts, her toe nails were painted red and on her feet she wore diamante studded sandals which complimented her long tanned legs; her beautifully made-up eyes appeared to be watching everyone in the room. As she lifted the tumbler to her lips the ice rattled in the glass.

"I wouldn't be surprised if she killed him," muttered Hetty, as Debbie returned and placed three glasses on the table, "She has guilt written all over her face."

"Hetty that's a dreadful thing to say," hissed Lottie. "Poor soul."

"Yes, it is a bit harsh, Het," Debbie dropped her purse into her handbag and then sat down.

"Besides which, she was in London shopping when Gavin was killed." Lottie could not hide the disdain for her sister's comment. "Remember, we heard all about it from Sid and Zac who got it from the pub's tradesmen they're working with."

"Ah, but was she in London? We only have her word for that."

Debbie smiled sweetly and attempted to alleviate the tension. "I think you'll find the police will have checked it out, Hetty. Next of kin are always the first suspects. And no doubt the life insurance company will have scrutinised her movements too. They don't pay up if they can help it."

Hetty's eyes were like saucers. "Did Gavin have life insurance then?"

Debbie nodded. "Yes, so I heard while in the post office yesterday morning. Apparently one of the tradesmen let it slip when he went in for some fags. He said it sympathetically though. You know, something along the lines of at least his poor widow will have some compensation and won't starve. I can't remember his exact words but it was something like that."

Hetty banged her fist down on the table and their glasses all shook. "Even more reason for her to have done him in then. I shall be keeping an eye on that one. Mark my word, ladies, I reckon she's as guilty as sin."

Chapter Twelve

"I've just come up from the village and there's a big notice outside the Crown and Anchor saying the pub's having a grand opening on Friday, July 12th so not long now as that's two weeks tomorrow," Kitty stood on the grass verge by the front boundary wall of Primrose Cottage and looked to where Hetty and Lottie sat in reclining garden chairs on the tarmac in front of their house, enjoying the morning sun.

"Thank goodness for that." Hetty removed her sunglasses so that she could clearly see their near neighbour.

"That's just what I said when I saw it. I'm not a big drinker but I've certainly missed the old place and so has Tommy."

"Care for a coffee?" Lottie asked, "It's getting a bit too warm sitting out here and Het and I were just thinking about having one anyway."

"Yes, why not. That would be very nice. Tom's out this morning playing bowls at Pentrillick House on the new green so he won't be back for an hour or two."

Hetty stood up. "We've talked about taking up bowls. It seems a nice leisurely sport for ladies of our years. Zac said we ought to go as he's keen for it to get plenty of use. As you know the green was Emma's idea and he's very supportive and proud of her."

"Oh, that's really sweet and yes, you should go then. In fact we all should. It would make a nice afternoon out." Kitty walked towards the gates and into the front garden.

"We shall then and we'll get Debbie to go with us too," Hetty removed her sunhat and dropped it onto her vacated chair.

"Your garden's really colourful. The best I've seen it since you've been living here."

Hetty bent to smell a scented rose by the door. "Well, there's a big incentive this year to have a good show. We don't expect to win but it's fun trying and it's keeping us on our toes. At the moment weeds get whipped out the minute they first appear."

"Anymore news as regards Gavin Snow's death, Kitty?" Lottie removed her sunglasses as they walked into the house.

"No, but someone said there's been another burglary. This time in St. Mary's Avenue."

Hetty's shoulders slumped. "Oh, no, I'd hoped whoever is responsible had moved further afield."

Lottie turned to face Kitty. "St. Mary's Avenue, that's where Debbie and Gideon live. Have you any idea which house it was?"

"No, but it wasn't Debbie and Gideon. Apparently it was someone who had been away on holiday and they found the place had been broken into when they arrived home last night. Meaning of course that we don't know when the robbery actually took place as the family have been away for a fortnight."

Lottie tutted. "Dreadful. I wonder why the Pentrillick area is being targeted."

Hetty went into the kitchen to make the coffee shaking her head and tutting; Lottie and Kitty sat down at the table in the sitting room.

"So how many robberies is that now, Kitty?"

"Three. Two were successful and in the third, which was actually the first, the robber escaped empty handed. That of course was the one in Honeysuckle Drive."

76

"Yes, the police mentioned that but they didn't say who he was. The person who was nearly robbed, I mean. Do you know him, Kitty?"

"Well, according to Tommy he's self-employed and is called Elliot Harris. I don't really know any more than that."

"Self-employed doing what?"

Kitty shrugged her shoulders. "Tommy wasn't sure but according to Bernie he has a taxi parked in the driveway so we assume he's a taxi driver."

Lottie shuddered. "Ugh! Not something I'd like to do."

"Me neither, the thought of driving people home in the early hours who've had one too many fills me with horror."

Hetty entered the room with three mugs on a tray and slices of cherry cake.

"I've been giving the robberies a bit of thought while making the coffee and I think whoever it is must be familiar with people's movements. So how might he achieve that?"

"That's what Tommy said and he reckons it must be someone living in the village who's a bit of a busybody."

"Or who has flappy ears," Hetty sat down.

"But I don't know of anyone who fits the description given out by the police, do you?" Lottie took a bite from her slice of cake.

Kitty shook her head. "No. I mean, lots of chaps are five tennish and of medium build and while it's unlikely that many people would notice a tattoo on someone's hand they're hardly going to miss a bloke with thick, dark brown curly hair. I mean, surely such a person would stick out like a sore thumb."

"That's just what I said to Het when we discussed it after the police called here."

"And don't forget the droopy moustache," said Hetty, "you don't see them very often these days."

Kitty laughed. "No, very nineteen seventies."

"Anyway, all I can say is I'm glad we have a dog. Albert might not be very fierce but hopefully his bark would be enough to scare away a potential burglar should we not be here one evening." Albert jumped from his basket on hearing his name, crossed the room and sat by Hetty's feet.

Kitty bent down and stroked the dog's head. "Well, what with one thing or another it's being quite an action packed summer this year, isn't it? What with the Pentrillick in Bloom competition, Vicar Sam getting married, the pub being done up, a series of robberies and of course a murder."

"Anymore news about that, Kitty?" Lottie asked, "The murder, I mean."

Hetty spoke before Kitty had a chance to answer. "I've already told you, Lottie, that it was the wife. I've given it a lot of thought and there's no question about it."

Lottie shook her head but did not respond verbally.

"What! You reckon it was Miranda?" Kitty was taken aback, "You've got to be kidding, Het."

"If Miranda is the name of Gavin's widow, then yes."

"No, don't be so silly. I've met her and she seemed a kindly soul."

"You've met her. When was that?" Hetty brushed cake crumbs into a small heap and picked them up between her thumb and forefinger.

"Yesterday. I was at the church arranging new flowers on the altar and when I came out with the old flowers to put them on the compost heap I saw her wandering around the graveyard. She smiled when she saw me, so I went over to her and we got chatting. She told me who she was and said she was looking for inspiration for when she had to choose a headstone for Gavin's grave."

Hetty's jaw dropped but she managed to refrain from making a snide remark.

On Friday afternoon, a gleaming BMW arrived in the village and swept into the newly tarmacked car park at the side of the Crown and Anchor. From it stepped a tall man with a straight back and a shock of jet black hair. From the boot of his car he took two suitcases and wheeled them into the pub. The first person he saw on entering the premises was Zac who was on his way out to Sid's van to fetch a piece of pipe.

Zac looked at the luggage and assumed the stranger was someone seeking accommodation. "Hi, I'm afraid the pub's not open yet, can I help you at all?"

"Yes, please. I'm looking for James and Ella Dale." The man's voice was rich and he spoke with an Italian accent.

"Benvolio," James having heard a familiar voice appeared from the dining room where a new floor was being laid, "Good to see you. Did you have a good journey?" The two men vigorously shook hands.

"Yes, fine, thank you, James. It took less time to get here than I'd anticipated, that's why I'm early."

James called to Zac who had turned towards the door. "Zac, I'm proud to say this is our new chef, Benvolio Moretti."

"Wow, you're Italian. I thought I recognised the accent. So does that mean there will be pizza on the menu?"

The new chef laughed. "Maybe, we shall see, Zac."

Benvolio Moretti was allocated an en suite room in the old part of the Crown and Anchor to be his for as long as he wanted. It was a lovely room which looked down onto the pub's sun terrace and the beach beyond. He realised it was also above the bar which at times might get a little noisy but as nine times out of ten he would most likely have a drink or two after he finished work he didn't think that would be an issue.

After he had unpacked his belongings and tried the bed for comfort, he sat down on a stool beside the window and watched as a small boat of anglers set sail from the shore.

"Well you've fallen on your feet with this job, Benvolio Moretti," he laughed, "A refreshing change from hotels and restaurants in the towns and cities. Might even find time for a bit of fishing and the occasional swim."

In the evening, James suggested they go to the Pentrillick Hotel for a meal so that the new chef could see what delicacies the opposition offered to their clientèle. After carefully studying the menu, Benvolio chose beer battered cod, chips, garden peas and homemade tartare sauce. "I can see by the look on your faces that you're surprised by my choice."

"Well, yes," admitted Ella. James nodded his agreement.

Benvolio laid down the menu and leaned back in his chair. "I'll tell you why I choose the fish and chips. It's because I spend much of my life in the kitchen experimenting with all types of exotic food, herbs and spices and so for me it's a treat to eat something humble and uncomplicated like fish and chips. What is more, I love it."

"Fair enough," James stood the menu back on its stand, "In fact I might even have the same."

"So will you be wanting to include fish and chips on the pub menu when we open?" Ella asked.

Benvolio shook his head. "No need. I noticed that you have a fish and chip shop in the village and it's on the menu here too. No, I'd like to do fish dishes but not in your traditional British way."

As they were leaving the dining room after their meal, Lottie, who was sitting in the adjoining bar with Hetty and Debbie enjoying Friday night drinks, saw them. "Look, look, that bloke over there with James and Ella. He must be the new chef," she whispered. "We saw young Zac earlier and he told us that he'd met him and that he's Italian, would you believe?"

Debbie chuckled. "Really! Well he certainly is a handsome brute. I bet he'll turn a few heads and probably break a few hearts."

"I suppose he is quite good looking," conceded Hetty.

"You suppose!" Debbie gasped, "If ever anyone lived up to the description tall, dark and handsome, it has to be him."

"Well, according to Zac he has a rich voice too," said Lottie, "so he might even be a good singer. You can't beat a good Italian tenor."

Debbie watched as the new chef sat down at the bar with the pub's licensees, then she turned to face Hetty and Lottie. "You mentioning singing has just reminded me of something. Gideon and I had a taxi the other day when we went to Marazion for a meal on our wedding anniversary and we hired the new chap who we saw has an advert in the post office window. I don't think you know him but he's called Elliot Harris and he's the bloke whose house was nearly robbed in Honeysuckle Drive."

"And who because he saw him was able to give a description of the burglar to the police," said Lottie, "Yes, we've heard about him but we've never met or even seen him for that matter. Kitty told us about him only yesterday and she said it was assumed he's a taxi driver because he has a taxi parked on his driveway."

"And now you've confirmed it so that's that little mystery solved." Hetty glanced at the window from which the sun was visible, setting in a blaze of colour.

"Anyway, we've interrupted you, haven't we, Debbie," apologised Lottie. "Sorry about that."

"That's okay, but where was I?"

Hetty turned her eyes away from the window and back into the room. "Going to Marazion in Elliot's taxi."

"Yes, of course. There's not much more to say, just that he not only took us there but he brought us back too and on hearing it was our wedding anniversary, he serenaded us with song all the way home."

"Really, oh that's so sweet," Lottie liked to hear accounts of good old fashioned romance.

"Well, it would have been but sadly he can't sing in tune so it reminded me of the good old days when Les Dawson played the piano. That was funny though but Elliot's singing set my teeth on edge."

"I can imagine and with Gideon being a big mover in the church choir I bet he suffered too."

Debbie chuckled. "Yes, poor Gideon. He says my singing is pretty poor but in comparison I'm Kiri Te Kanawa."

An hour later as the ladies walked out of the hotel's main entrance, a taxi pulled up alongside the kerb on the opposite side of the road.

"Well I'll be blowed! Talk of the devil, that's Elliot's taxi," stated Debbie, "Funny I only mentioned him a short while ago."

Standing at the bottom of the hotel steps they watched as Elliot sprang from the driver's seat and opened the back door of his taxi. From it he helped out a clearly inebriated woman who stumbled in her very high heeled shoes. She opened her handbag, gave Elliot a small bundle of notes and told him to keep the change. He thanked her and then escorted her across the road and up the steps, through the hotel's open door and into the vestibule, acknowledging the three dumbfounded ladies as he did so.

"Well, I never," spluttered Hetty, "Now do you believe me when I say that Miranda Snow is no grieving widow?"

Chapter Thirteen

"There are tiny green tomatoes on my plants now," Bill spoke with pride as the family sat round the dining room table for breakfast on Monday morning, "I reckon by the time the competition is judged they'll be smothered in delicious rosy red fruit."

"Yes, they're certainly looking healthy," conceded Sandra, "I have to admit I'm impressed."

Bill beamed with pride. "A chap I work with bought some at the same time as me and he told us yesterday that his have all died."

Vicki yawned. It seemed the conversation every morning during breakfast included a progress report on her father's hanging baskets and she half-wished someone would pinch them both. She knew that was unlikely though for Bill had securely padlocked the baskets to the brackets from which they hung.

In the afternoon, Debbie drove to Blackberry Way where she picked up Hetty, Lottie and Kitty. Their destination was Pentrillick House for a game of bowls.

"I haven't the foggiest idea how to play," confessed Hetty as she fastened her seatbelt, "Have any of you?"

Kitty and Lottie both shook their heads.

"I only know that we need to wear flat rubber soled shoes so we don't damage the grass," said Kitty, "and I must say these new trainers are really comfortable. As a keen walker I wish I'd bought some years ago."

"I couldn't agree more. I feel quite trendy." Lottie looked down with delight at the gleaming white shoes on her feet.

Debbie started the engine. "I Googled bowls last night but it didn't make much sense. Something about a Jack or a Kitty and it mentioned rinks whatever they might be. There are different types of greens too and I've no idea which they have at Pentrillick House."

"I think you'll find there will be someone there to advise us how to play," Kitty reassured them. "Tommy did tell me who it is but I've forgotten."

Debbie pulled out of Blackberry Way and turned into Long Lane. "It's Sally Oliver, she's the instructor. You know who I mean. She and her husband Robert moved to the village earlier this year and live in the flat over the charity shop. Gideon speaks well of them, especially Robert because he works with him."

"Yes, of course, I remember now. They're the really nice couple who came up with the idea of a gardening club." From the back seat of the car, Kitty waved to a member of the church choir out walking her dog. "When I told Tommy we were going to try our hands at bowls he said we ought to get a few teams together and have competitions. I think that sounds fun."

"Yes, that's a lovely idea. How many in a team?" Hetty asked.

Kitty pulled a face. "I forgot to ask."

Debbie waited at the junction for a bus to pass. "Now I can answer that because it was one part of the description I did understand. Apparently it varies but four is the most common number."

"Perfect," Lottie laughed. "We are a team already then."

"Is Sally the only instructor at the bowling green or are there others?" Hetty asked.

"I believe at present she's the only one," said Kitty, "so fingers crossed she'll be working this afternoon."

"Well if she is there that means we'll see her twice in one day," chuckled Hetty, "because having come up with the idea she's bound to be at the gardening club's first meeting tonight."

Sid and Zac having finished the plumbing work at the Crown and Anchor on Monday morning, returned to the new housing estate in the afternoon to continue their work there.

"Ah, it's good to be back again," Sid put down his tool box, "It was nice working in the pub but here we're our own bosses and this is our job not someone else's."

Zac walked over to the window and looked out onto rubble that covered an area which one day would be someone's garden. "I agree. I really love being up here. It's near to everything yet tucked away at the same time. In fact I wish one of these houses could be mine. Just a little one for me and Emma."

Sid was touched by the wistful tone of Zac's voice. "Why don't you put your names down then? You'd have nothing to lose."

Zac turned away from the window. "Do you think we'd stand a chance? I mean, we're not married or homeless and we don't have any kids so I hardly think we'd qualify."

"No, but the houses are for local people and you both live in the village and so do your parents. Your mum works at the care home here, Emma works at Pentrillick House and your work is based here too. Emma also went to the village school. If you want to live together then one of these houses would be the ideal solution. What does Emma think about it?"

Zac shrugged his shoulders. "I don't know; it's not something we've ever discussed. I mean, we believe we were made for each other but that's as far as it's ever got. At the moment Emma's wrapped up with her new job and we've been pretty busy too this summer, haven't we? So as it stands we've not given any thought to the future."

"Yes, we have been busy but that's no reason to neglect your personal life. I suggest you have a word with Emma and take it from there. But don't leave it too late because these houses will be ready for occupation in two or three months' time."

"Thanks, Sid. I'll do that when the time seems right."

At seven o'clock that evening the gardening club met for the first time in the village hall; the meeting was chaired by Sally Oliver. No plants were involved, the get-together was purely to toy over ideas for the following weeks. In all, twenty people were present and other names were mentioned of interested parties unable to attend the first meeting. Shortly after the meeting began, Clara Bragg arrived and apologised for her lateness.

"I'm so sorry, but because I had the afternoon off work I popped over to Camborne to see a friend and cut it a bit fine to get back on time and then would you believe, when I was nearly here I got stuck behind a tractor for a couple of miles."

"Oh, I can quite believe that," laughed Sally, "it happens to us frequently."

Most of the gardening enthusiasts nodded their agreement. Pleased that she had received a warm welcome, Clara took the nearest free seat available which was at the back next to Bill.

After a brief debate it was decided to keep the name of the group simple and so members opted for Pentrillick Gardening Club. The purpose of the club would be to celebrate the mild Cornish climate, to exchange tips, make new friends and discuss ideas that might improve the village from a horticultural point of view. It was also suggested they visit gardens open to the public in the county at least once a month.

"Are we going to elect a committee?" asked Clara.

"That's a very good point," acknowledged Sally, "I would like to think that meetings be as laid back as possible but the hall has to be paid for and trips organised and so forth. We might even invite a guest speaker from time to time. What do you all think?"

"How much does the hall cost?" Kitty asked.

"Ten pounds an hour for just the main hall or fifteen pounds if we also hire the kitchen."

After further discussion it was unanimously agreed that the group elect a committee. And after persuasion by members, Sally was eventually nominated and elected as chairperson. Shortly after, Tess was elected as secretary and Veronica the treasurer. It was also agreed they have six further committee members who were, Clara, Robert, Bill, Tommy, Maisie and Kitty. Once the elections had taken place, Sally asked if there were any more questions or suggestions.

Veronica raised her hand. "Do you think we might offer a service to people who are unable to tend their own gardens? On a voluntary basis, that is. I'm not talking landscaping. Just grass cutting, weeding and hedge trimming for the elderly and the infirm."

Kitty wrung her hands with delight. "That's a lovely idea, Veronica. There must be a lot of people who can no longer look after what was once their pride and joy."

Lottie nodded. "I agree but might people not be offended if we suggest to them that their gardens need tending? After all some people don't seem to care or notice if their gardens are an eyesore."

Collective laughter filled the room before Veronica answered. "I'm not suggesting we force them into it. I'm thinking more along the lines of putting out flyers to any house that looks in need of a little TLC."

"It still might cause offence if we're selective," reasoned Sally, "and we don't want to get off to a bad start and be labelled as overbearing."

"Then we must drop flyers through every letterbox in the village to avoid that," stated Hetty, "And in particular the bungalow near to Sea View Cottage. I don't know who lives there but the garden is getting to be quite an eyesore."

"Yes, it is," Kitty acknowledged, "Betsy Triggs lives there. She's a widow who lost her husband a couple of years back. She's elderly, suffers with arthritis and doesn't get out much. It was her husband who did the garden and she isn't fit enough, health wise, to tackle it."

"Then we must help her," said Veronica, "Perhaps someone could call on her and offer our services."

Kitty looked doubtful. "I think it might be best if we did as Hetty suggested and drop off flyers to every house in the village then if she mentions it to anyone they'll be able to say they've received one too. She's a very independent lady and I'd hate her to think that we were critical of her garden and had picked her out. She also has a sharp tongue."

"Fair enough," agreed Veronica.

"Right, so is it agreed by all that we'll print off flyers and deliver one to every household in the village, especially to the home of Betsy Triggs and other houses where the elderly live who might seem unable to cope with their gardens?" Sally asked.

All members raised their hands to demonstrate their approval.

"Excellent." Sally addressed Kitty, "Do you know what Betsy's house is called?"

"I believe it's Sunnyside."

"It is," Hetty confirmed, "I noticed the name on the gate the other day when we came out of church."

"If we give flyers to everyone then surely we'll get bone idle people asking for help who are neither elderly nor infirm," suggested Tess.

"Good point," agreed Sally, "how do we overcome that?"

"By emphasising the words *elderly* and *infirm*," said Kitty, "I think that should be enough and if we do get any enquiries then it must be for the committee to decide whether or not applicants qualify."

Tess raised her hand. "It's just occurred to me but might it not be a good idea to also put an advert in the Pentrillick Gazette offering our services to the elderly and infirm?"

"Excellent suggestion," agreed Sally, "and at the same time we can let it be known that new members are always welcome to join us."

Kitty's husband, Tommy chuckled. "Thinking about old folks, it's only just hit me, but at what age do we consider someone to be elderly? I ask because several of us here are pensioners, over sixty or both."

"As am I, Tommy," laughed Sally, "as am I. So I think we must leave that definition for the time being and judge each case on its merit."

Tess, the newly elected secretary, volunteered to print the flyers and pen an advertisement for the Pentrillick Gazette. At the end of the meeting members mingled with mugs of coffee and cakes made by Sally and Veronica.

Clara Bragg made a beeline for Bill as he made his way towards the kitchen counter. She tapped his arm. "I've seen you with Sandra. Are you her husband?"

Bill turned around. "Yes, I am and she would have been here tonight but she's working. Hopefully she'll be able to come next week though because she does love her garden."

"Yes, I know she's working because we work at the same place and she said she was sorry she'd not be here tonight." Clara picked up a cup of coffee and took a sip, "So, are you a keen gardener, Bill? I think your name's Bill?"

"Yes, it is, and yes I am. No, actually that's not really true. I don't really do any gardening I leave that to Sandra but I am in charge of our hanging baskets for the Pentrillick in Bloom competition." Bill spoke with pride.

Clara attempted to smoother a smile. "Oh, yes, I've heard what happened to your original basket. Most unfortunate, especially for poor Gavin Snow."

On Tuesday morning, inspired by the first meeting of the Gardening Club, members not working, enthusiastically tended their gardens, took cuttings and split plants to share with other members. Tess, in her new position as secretary, looked on-line at gardens in West Cornwall that were open to the public and the costs of hiring a coach. She then wrote a brief draft for the flyer and when she was satisfied with its content, printed off copies.

Meanwhile, on the new housing estate, Sid and Zac finished work mid-afternoon as they were unable to continue until the next delivery of bathroom suites would arrive the following morning.

Pleased that he was able to finish work early, Zac rang Emma to see what she was doing. To his delight she had the day off work and so they agreed to meet on the beach at four o'clock.

Emma was already there when Zac arrived freshly showered with towel tucked beneath his arm. He sat down beside her on a blanket and kissed her lightly on the cheek. "So what have you been doing all day while I've been slaving over hot taps and pipes?"

"Not much. I tidied my bedroom this morning and then made a cake for Claire's birthday. I can't believe my little sister is ten tomorrow. It seems like only yesterday that she was born."

"Yes, and now you're a grown up lady of twenty."

"I don't know about the grown up bit but I'm certainly twenty."

"Em, I've been thinking. I mean you might not like my idea but…" He then told her of his thoughts of sharing a house together. His words spilled out quickly fearing that he might not have a chance to express everything that he felt and wanted to say. To his amazement, she placed her hand gently over his mouth. "Shush. You don't need to say anymore, Zac. I think it's a lovely idea. In fact the same thoughts had crossed my mind too."

"Really!" Zac was overcome with emotion.

"Yes, but as it is I see there are two obstacles in our way: one, we might not get a house anyway, and two…"

"…our parents," finished Zac.

"Yes, I know they can't stop us applying because we're both over eighteen but I should hate to go against their wishes. My parents have been very good to me and yours to you. Having said that, I know my parents are keen for me to be independent and they never treat me like a child."

Zac looked thoughtful. "Yes, you're quite right and my parents treat me as an adult too. Most of the time anyway. I suggest we see what they say and then take it from there."

Emma stood up. "Yes, meanwhile let's go for a swim."

Zac sprang to his feet. "I'm game. Race you to the rocks and back."

Emma removed the shirt covering her bikini and tossed it onto the blanket. "You're on and I propose whoever comes last pays for tonight's Chinese takeaway."

Chapter Fourteen

On Tuesday evening, after several pints of beer with Bill in the hotel bar, Norman took the stairs to his room on the second floor and carried out his usual nightly routine before retiring to bed. Because the night was warm he opened the window fully to let in a gentle breeze then sat on the cushioned window seat overlooking the gardens, partly illuminated by a light above the hotel's name board.

As the church clock struck midnight he was convinced that he saw the shadow of a person lurking in the shrubbery. Unable to see clearly he switched off the bedside lights to improve visibility and then returned to the window to take a second look. As he sat he heard a sudden snap reminiscent of a twig breaking and then the upper foliage of a golden privet bush shuddered. Norman calculated that the movement was too high up to have been caused by a cat or a dog and was more likely the result of a human being brushing against the leaves. Alarm bells rang in his mind as it occurred to him that if it were a person hiding amongst the shrubbery then he or she might possibly be Pentrillick's notorious burglar. To put his mind at rest, Norman called out, "Is there anyone down there?" No-one answered, all was silent and there were no more movements. Norman laughed. No doubt the fact that he and Bill had been joined in the bar by Bill's mother, aunt and their friend, Debbie after the ladies had played bingo in the village hall, and that the conversation had been dominated by stories of ghosts and the recent murder, had left his mind over-active. Happy with that thought, he stood up; at the same time a car pulled up on the opposite side of the road. Realising it was a taxi, Norman watched as from the driver's seat stepped a tall man with a shaven head. He opened the back door of the vehicle and helped out a young woman, whom he recognised as Miranda Snow. She paid the driver who escorted her across the road and through the open gates of the hotel out of Norman's field of vision. In less than a minute the taxi driver was back in his sight, whistling tunelessly as he crossed the road. Norman watched as he stepped into his vehicle and drove away. Amused by the tottering state of the young widow, he left the window open and climbed into bed.

After breakfast the following morning, Norman left the hotel to buy flowers to put on the graves of his deceased relatives resting in the churchyard. As he passed by the shrubbery he paused and looked over his shoulder. Hoping that he could not be seen, he walked over to where he thought he had seen movement the previous evening. A few dry twiglets lay on the earth amongst fallen leaves and dead fuchsia flower heads but there was no trace of anyone having been there. No broken branches on the shrubs or footsteps in the earth but then the earth was so hard and dry it was unlikely that footsteps would show up anyway. Glad that he must have been mistaken, he continued on his way.

In the afternoon, Hetty, Lottie and Debbie collected flyers from Tess, who was working in Taffeta's Tea Shoppe, to distribute around the village.

"I've done two hundred, I hope that's enough," Tess reached beneath the counter for a carrier bag.

"Should be," said Lottie, "we won't put them through letterboxes where gardens are well tended so that should save a few."

"We won't deliver them to members of the Gardening Club either," Hetty added, "so that'll save a few more."

"Well, good luck and let's hope we're able to help someone."

"So what have you written?" Debbie asked.

"Look and see," Tess handed over the bag.

Debbie read,

The newly formed Pentrillick Gardening Club is delighted to offer a free of charge service to the elderly and infirm in the village who are unable to tend their own gardens. Jobs undertaken are weeding, grass cutting and hedge trimming. Should you be eligible or know of someone who is then please get in touch.

The flyer concluded with the names, phone numbers and email addresses of three committee members: the chairperson, the secretary and the treasurer.

"What about the advert for the Gazette?" Hetty asked, "Are you doing that too, Tess?"

"Yes, but there's no rush as the July edition is already out and the August one won't be printed for another three weeks."

Lottie tutted. "I can't believe we're in July already. The schools break up soon and then when they go back it'll be the Christmas term. And it doesn't seem many minutes since the lights went up last Christmas."

"I agree," said Debbie, "we all seem to have such busy lives now and for some reason it makes time go quicker."

Hetty laughed. "Except that it doesn't, does it? There are still twenty four hours in a day, seven days in a week and twelve months in a year. So in reality nothing has changed."

Lottie picked up the bag of flyers. "No but a year now is a sixty seventh of our lives, Het, whereas when we were six it was a sixth. Hence a year seems to go much quicker."

On Wednesday evening, inside her room at the Pentrillick Hotel, Miranda Snow pushed up the sash window, leaned out and took in a deep breath of the clean, fresh, sea air. The evening was warm with a gentle breeze blowing up from the south east and the scent of honeysuckle twisted around a wooden trellis on the wall beside her window filled the evening with its glorious fragrance. Bewitched by her surroundings, she leaned her elbows on the bottom of the window frame and listened to the gentle rhythmic sound of the sea just visible, sparkling in the evening sunlight. When her arms began to ache, she part-closed the window, went into the bathroom, turned on the bath taps and sprinkled crystals into the flowing water. From a dish she took a box of matches, lit an array of scented candles sporadically placed around the room and then closed the blind to shut out the light. To silence the humdrum noise, she turned off the extractor fan and watched as the full length mirror steamed up and blurred her reflection. She then undressed keeping a watchful eye on the bathwater as it rose and foamed. When the tub was nearly full she turned off the taps, stepped into the bath, slipped beneath the bubbles and relaxed in the warm scented water.

As the candles flickered around the room, she poured a large glass of white wine from a bottle in a bucket of ice on the tiled floor. Popular tunes wafted in through the partly open bathroom door from a music channel on the television set which hung on the wall opposite her bed.

From the bathmat, Miranda picked up her mobile phone and spoke when she heard her friend answer. "Hi Patty, I thought I'd better ring and bring you up to date. There have been further developments since we met in Truro last night."

There was a pause while Patty spoke and then Miranda giggled.

"Yes, it was brilliant, wasn't it? We really ought not to drink so much though. I felt as rough as rats this morning. Anyway, the reason I'm ringing, apart from wanting to hear your voice that is, is because I heard from the insurance company today and guess what? Yes, they're going to pay up but it'll be a few more weeks yet." There was a pause. "I knew you'd be thrilled and I don't know about you but I think it's time to plan a holiday, after the funeral of course."

While Miranda laughed at Patty's response, the partly open window in her bedroom slid wide open. And as she continued to chat and laugh with eyes closed dreamily, she was unaware that the music from the television had increased in volume and that the candles around the room were flickering wildly in the draught from the gaping bedroom window.

Without opening her eyes, Miranda tilted her head forwards and took another sip of wine, she then leaned back and listened further to the cheery voice of her friend. It was not until she heard a cough that she opened her eyes and saw a dark shadow outside the bathroom door. Realising something was amiss, she sat up. Water dripped from the ends of her short blonde hair. Her heart rate increased, goose pimples rose on her wet, bare arms and her wine glass clinked as she placed it on the edge of the bathtub.

"P...P...Patty, I'll call you back," she whispered, "I need to check something out."

She dropped the phone onto the floor and as she attempted to stand and reach for the towel, the bathroom door was flung wide open and a person dressed from head to toe in black stepped into the room. Only his eyes were visible; the rest of his face and head were concealed beneath a black balaclava.

"You," she gasped.

"I'm flattered that you recognise me. I suppose it's my gorgeous eyes." He fluttered his eyelashes teasingly.

Miranda slid back down into the scented water. "How did you know where to find me?"

"Fate. You see I never gave up looking. I knew our paths would cross again one day."

"Please go."

"Oh, I will but only when I'm ready."

"But…but…what do you want?" Her voice trembled as she spoke.

"You're about to find out."

He took off his gloves, tossed them onto the floor, stepped nearer to the bath and dropped down onto his knees. Panic-stricken Miranda sat up straight and opened her mouth to scream, but before she was able to utter a sound her head was forced back hard against the ceramic tub. She struggled as he clamped his right hand firmly over her mouth and water spilled over the side of the bath as his other hand pressed down her raised legs. With determination she fought for her life but it was all in vain for he was too strong and with a mighty splash she felt herself pushed down into the water, where submerged beneath the scented bubbles she was held until her struggling ceased.

Chapter Fifteen

"Have you heard the latest?" Debbie spoke quickly as Lottie picked up the phone in the hallway of Primrose Cottage.

"Latest? I don't know what you mean. Het and I haven't seen anyone since yesterday when we gave out the flyers."

Lottie listened in disbelief as Debbie told of the gruesome discovery at the Pentrillick Hotel. As she put down the receiver and turned towards the living room to relay the news to Hetty, the doorbell rang. On the doorstep stood Vicar Sam and his new wife, Martha.

"Oh, you're back. How lovely. Do come in." Lottie stepped aside to let the newlyweds in. "So how was the honeymoon?"

"Wonderful," gushed Martha, "Italy has never looked better and the weather was superb."

Lottie closed the door. "Oh, I am pleased for you both and you'll be able to discuss your holiday with the pub's new chef when you meet him because we're told that he's an Italian."

Martha's eyes shone. "Really! That's fantastic, I shall look forward to that. Have you any idea which part of Italy he comes from?"

Lottie shook her head; she felt flustered. "Sorry, I'm afraid not."

"When is the Crown and Anchor is due to reopen?" Vicar Sam asked, "It seems to have been closed for ages."

"Friday, July the 12th and we can't wait to see what's been done there."

Lottie led them into the sitting room where Hetty was already standing to greet them.

"Please take a seat." The newlyweds sat close together on the couch. "Tea?" Hetty asked.

Martha smiled. "Well, actually, please don't be offended, but we'd rather not. We're visiting all our wedding guests who live in the village today to thank them for their wonderful gifts and so we've already drunk far more tea than we ought."

Hetty sat down. "Say no more." She turned to Lottie. "I'm sure Sam and Martha won't mind me asking but who on earth was that on the phone just now? You're clearly upset about something."

Not wanting to gossip, Lottie looked uncomfortable. "It was Debbie and I'm afraid, Het that she had bad news."

Hetty's eyebrows rose.

Vicar Sam leaned forwards. "Would you like us to leave?"

"No, no, not at all," Lottie waved her hand to indicate they should stay seated. "It's just that Miranda Snow is dead."

"Dead!" Hetty was shocked.

"Was the lady a friend of yours?" Martha asked.

"No, no, we didn't even know her. She's the widow of the plumber who was brutally killed in the churchyard." Lottie tried to stop her hands from shaking. "I don't suppose you've heard about that yet."

"Well, actually, we have," admitted the young vicar, "We heard about it while we were away. At first Vicar George was reluctant to tell us but the police said that he ought to and so he eventually rang a few days after it had happened. Bless him, he was so apologetic and said that it was all in hand and that we weren't to worry about a thing."

Martha nodded, "Yes that's right and then dear Kitty rang last night to welcome us home and she filled us in with the details, didn't she, Sam?"

"She did and now you say his poor widow has passed away," Sam was clearly shocked.

"So sad. Did the poor lady die from a broken heart, I wonder?" Martha squeezed her husband's hand.

Hetty turned to her sister. "How did she die, Lottie? Was it natural causes?"

Lottie squirmed in discomfort. "No, no, sadly I'm afraid not. You see, she was found drowned in the bath and rumour has it that it might have been suicide."

"Suicide!" Hetty wanted to say that she very much doubted that as the young widow was about to come into a substantial amount of money and looked anything but grief stricken but instead she said, "How sad and not a very good homecoming for you is it, Vicar?"

Sensing that he was shocked, Martha replied on Sam's behalf. "We must visit the poor lady's next of kin. Were there any children, do you know?"

Lottie shook her head. "No, there are no children and I don't know anything of her next of kin. All we do know is that she came from Bodmin, worked in a bank but we don't know which one, and was down here waiting for her husband's body to be released for burial."

After Vicar Sam and Martha left to visit more parishioners, Hetty and Lottie took mugs of tea out into the back garden where they sat in the sun on a bench beside their pond.

"I really don't know what to make of this latest piece of news, Het. I mean, why on earth would Miranda commit suicide?"

"Goodness only knows and of course knowing very little about her it's difficult to even make a wild guess."

"I agree, it is. I mean if what we've heard is true and she was about to get a hefty pay-out from the insurance company then she certainly had no money worries and as you've pointed out on several occasions she never seemed overly distressed by the loss of Gavin. Even I have to concede that."

Hetty drained her mug and placed it on the arm of the bench. "Perhaps it wasn't suicide. Perhaps someone got into her room and drowned her."

Lottie shook her head. "No, I can't see that being the case because she doesn't know anyone here, does she?"

"True, but then nor did Gavin other than his work colleagues."

"He knew James and Ella and of course he was here long enough to get to know some of the locals too. Sid for instance, they often used to chat and there were no doubt others."

"Yes, of course but as regards Miranda we'll just have to wait until we hear a bit more. It gives me the creeps though. What with a murder, burglaries and now a suicide, suddenly things are not going too well this summer." Hetty felt downcast.

"Oh hang on, I've just thought of something, Het. Remember when we were leaving the hotel last Friday we saw her come back in a taxi."

Hetty nodded. "Yes, but what of it?"

"Well, she'd obviously been somewhere drinking and she'd had too much judging by the state of her. Now if you think about it, it's unlikely that she would bother to leave the hotel just to drink alone and so she must have met up with someone somewhere down here."

Hetty sat up straight. "Good point. We need to look into this, Lottie. I wonder if the taxi driver would tell us where she'd been."

"I don't think he would because he doesn't even know us, does he? He might tell Debbie though after all he did serenade her and Gideon on their wedding anniversary."

"True, but we won't say anything just yet. I suggest we wait until we've heard whether or not Miranda's death was suicide

101

because there's no point looking for a motive and so forth if she took her own life."

"You're right, Het and hopefully she did because the thought of another murder is too horrendous to contemplate."

Since the end of April, every other morning as soon as it was light, Sally Oliver crept out of the flat and tried not to disturb Robert if he was still sleeping. She then walked down to the beach for a swim. It was something she had done for many years but at her previous address the activity had taken place at a pool not far from their home. At first Sally was apprehensive about swimming in the sea. Not because she was afraid of the waves or the fact there would be no-one around; it was the temperature of the water that sourced her doubt. For although the morning air might be warm when the sun rose, the water always struck her as cold and she wasn't surprised to learn that the difference in the sea's temperature between winter and summer was only a few degrees.

On Thursday morning she had gone down to the beach as normal, the tide was out and as usual there was no-one around. But already there was warmth in the sun and its rays caused the sea to sparkle as far as the eye could see. Sally walked across the beach to her usual place where she removed her outer garments and placed them on a bench along with her towel. She then walked down to the water's edge and waded into the gentle waves. She swam back and forth for thirty minutes and stopped only when she heard the church clock strike six thirty. She then swam towards the shore but as she passed over rocks her foot caught on something beneath the waves. Keeping herself afloat she reached down to see what the something was. To her surprise it was a rope. Not wanting anyone else to become entangled in it she swam towards the shore with one end of the rope firmly held in her hand. Once on the sand she pulled its entire length from the water. The rope was long and strong and she felt it must have been lost at some point by a boat out in the Channel or maybe it had been washed out to sea somewhere along the coast. Unsure what to do with it, she wound it into a coil and placed it by the boats which stood at the top of the beach hoping by doing so that someone might make good use of it. She then dried herself, got dressed and feeling invigorated went home for breakfast and to prepare for a day's work at the bowling green in the grounds of Pentrillick House.

Late on Friday afternoon, James and Ella Dale said goodbye to Vince, Leo and Max. Their work at the Crown and Anchor was finished and it was time for them to pack up all the tools, and their belongings from the caravans and return to Bodmin.

"It'll be strange not having the chaps around;" Ella waved as the three vans left the new car park and drove off along the main street, "and so sad for them to leave knowing their late workmate's widow has taken her own life."

"I agree, sweetheart. Sadly, thoughts of their work here will always be overshadowed by bad memories."

Ella turned and looked lovingly at the pub. "And now the work for us begins."

"Yes, there's a lot to do between now and our opening next Friday. I just hope we can fit it all in."

"Oh, I'm sure we will. Neither of us is afraid of hard work and it'll certainly be nice to get the kitchen stocked up and the shelves in the bar too."

James rubbed his hands together. "And beer in the pumps. That's what I'm looking forward to, my sweet. You can't beat a glass of draught real ale."

They turned and with arms linked went back inside the pub. "So when do we open the champagne? Are we leaving it until the grand opening?"

James grinned. "What do you think? I mean no time like the present and with the building work being completed we have just reached a milestone."

Ella bit her bottom lip. "It's rather early in the day but I must admit I do feel like celebrating."

"That's my girl," James kissed her cheek, "You go and fetch the champers from the fridge and I'll get Benvolio from the dining room. That's if I can tear him away from creating the opening week's menus."

Ten minutes later, with champagne flutes in hand, James, Ella and Benvolio were out on the pub's sun terrace. "Here's to success and hopefully many, many happy years of running this wonderful pub," said James.

"Hear, hear," cried Ella and Benvolio together.

They chinked and raised their glasses and then sat down in the afternoon sun to relish the days that lay ahead.

On Friday evening, Ivor and Sophie Shepherd went to the Pentrillick Hotel for a meal to celebrate Sophie's twenty ninth birthday. After the meal they went into the bar and got chatting to Bill, having a drink with Norman who was due to go home the following Monday.

"How are you liking life in Pentrillick?" Bill asked, as the Shepherds joined them on the bar stools.

Ivor sucked in his breath. "Well now, that's a tricky one. I mean, we like the village well enough, we love being by the sea and the people are really friendly. But what with the burglaries and the fact that there have been two shocking deaths, both of which I attended, and this in the first six weeks of our being here, I'm not sure how to answer your question."

Bill nodded. "Fair enough, so let's change the subject and I'll introduce you to Norman here whose family used to own and live in the Old Bakehouse which of course is now our home."

Norman leaned forwards and shook hands with the Shepherds in turn.

"So do you live locally now?" Sophie asked, "Because I'm sure I've seen you before."

"No, I lived here in the village until I was two, not that I can remember it, but now I'm just visiting. You probably saw me a few weeks back although it was only a flying visit when I was here for the wedding of my niece."

"Oh, so it was your niece who married the vicar?"

Norman nodded. "Yes, our Martha married Vicar Sam and what a smashing bloke he is."

"So we've heard," Ivor acknowledged.

Sophie's eyes sparkled. "That will be when I saw you then because we watched the wedding party leave the church and so forth." She closed her eyes, "If I remember correctly you were wearing a grey suit, light yellow shirt and an orange tie."

"Good grief. Yes, that was me. Fancy you remembering that."

"Sophie is very observant," laughed Ivor, "meaning I can't get away with much."

"So what brings you to the village this time?" Sophie stretched to ease her back.

"Well funnily enough it's because I'm thinking of moving back down here and have my sights set on one of the houses being built on the new estate."

"Really! We could well be neighbours in the future then because Ivor and I are thinking of buying one too. Aren't we, love?"

"Hmm, yes, providing there are no more murders in the village." Ivor pointed to an empty table in an alcove. "Shall we all go and sit over there? I can see your back's aching, Soph."

Sophie stood up. "Yes, that's a good idea. I find high stools get uncomfortable after a while."

Norman nodded. "I have to agree with you there."

They all lifted their glasses and walked across the bar towards the empty table.

"Right, now where were we?" Bill asked as they all took seats.

Ivor moved his chair as the setting sun was in his eyes. "I had just agreed with Sophie that we're thinking of buying one of the new houses."

Sophie laughed, "But then you rather spoiled it by adding that's providing there are no more murders in the village."

"Spot on: you did," agreed Norman.

"And there may actually only have been one anyway," added Bill, "as it's rumoured that Miranda Snow's death was most likely suicide."

"Or she might even have had a heart attack or a stroke or an aneurism," reasoned Norman, "the list is endless."

Ivor shook his head. "No, it's definitely two murders. I heard at work today that according to the coroner bruises on her legs and mouth indicate that she was pushed and held down in the bath. It'll be made public tomorrow morning."

"She was murdered," Norman felt his heart beat increase as he recalled sensing that someone was hiding in the shrubbery on the evening before Miranda Snow died. To ease his conscience, he made a mental note to inform the police before breakfast the following morning.

Chapter Sixteen

On Monday morning, Norman checked out of the Pentrillick Hotel as planned for he wanted to get home to get the purchase of one of the new houses rolling with his solicitor and see how things were going with the sale of his own house. However, before he left he made a single room reservation for the last weekend of July as he wanted to be back in the village for the judging of the Pentrillick in Bloom competition.

On Monday evening, the Gardening Club held its second meeting and Sandra who had worked the previous week and so missed the first meeting was looking forward to seeing how things were progressing. As before the chairs were in rows. She and Bill sat on the second row. As they chatted to Tess in the row behind them, Clara arrived and made a beeline for the empty chair next to Bill. She promptly slapped his thigh. "I'm glad you're here again, Billy. How are your hanging baskets doing? Still got them?"

Sandra leaned forwards and scowled at the new arrival.

"Oh, hi, Sandra, I didn't realise it was you sitting there. For some reason I thought you were working tonight."

"I was meant to be," she hissed, "but I swapped shifts so that I could be here." Her smile was through gritted teeth.

Bill, unsure how to react decided to play safe and announced that he needed to go to the Gents. Sandra continued to glare and then resumed her conversation with Tess, who was clearly amused by the brief encounter.

Shortly after, the meeting began. Sally welcomed everyone and especially the few new faces amongst the members. She then said that she was very pleased to announce that four people had asked for the Gardening Club's help and one of them was Betsy Triggs, and because Betsy was the first to ask it was agreed that her garden be the one they tackled first. After informing members of the work that needed to be done as assessed by Robert and herself who had been along to Sunnyside to meet Betsy, she asked for volunteers to attend the clearance and for the meeting to set a day on which the work would take place. To Sandra's annoyance, when Bill realised the work at Betsy's house would be on his day off he volunteered to help and straight away, Clara volunteered too. Not to be outdone, Sandra said she would also be there even though she knew it meant swapping shifts again. Other volunteers were Sally, Tommy and Tess. Debbie would have liked to help too but she had a dental appointment that day. Hetty and Lottie with all the time in the world also volunteered but not for the heavy work. They were allocated the job of providing refreshments for the workers.

"Friday's going to be a busy day," said Hetty to Lottie as they walked home after the meeting, "because in the evening the pub will be opening its doors at last so it's just as well we're not doing any strenuous work or we'd probably fall asleep after the first glass of wine."

"Bring it on," shouted Lottie, "I reckon that going to Betsy's and then later to the pub's opening will make Friday the best day of the week."

"Probably even the best day of the year," laughed Hetty.

On Tuesday afternoon, Hetty and Lottie sauntered down to the village to visit the family at the Old Bakehouse; en route they sat down on the bus stop bench to watch the world go by.

Lottie glanced up at the clock on the church tower. "We have ten minutes 'til the next bus is due so we must be gone by then as we don't want the driver to stop for nothing."

"Good point although he probably wouldn't stop anyway if we weren't standing with our arms out."

"No, I suppose not and someone might even get off here."

Hetty patted the arm of the bench. "I think there ought to be more seats along the road here. It's nice just to sit and watch people go by and the traffic too as we don't see much of either up in Blackberry Way."

From where they sat they could see Sunnyside and the overgrown state of Betsy Triggs's garden.

"Funny, I've never really noticed Betsy's garden before," said Lottie, "but then I suppose it's because we always walk on this side of the road. You know, for the church, the village hall and the hotel."

"And the Old Bakehouse," Hetty added.

"Yes, of course."

"I only noticed a few weeks ago when we took the bus into Helston for a change. If you remember we sat upstairs and so I looked down on it. You sat on the opposite side of the aisle to me though so you wouldn't have been able to see it."

"I wonder what she's like and if we've ever seen her before."

Hetty looked towards the bungalow where only its roof was visible above the trees and shrubs. "Yes, I've thought that too. We know from Kitty that she has a sharp tongue and is a widow but that's about all."

"Might be a bit of a harridan then."

"Hopefully not as we'll be indoors with her making the teas and coffees. Anyway, I think Sally liked her by the way she spoke at the meeting last night, so she can't be too bad."

"I don't think I'd like to live where she is. Too many places to hide." The thought of being surrounded by overgrown vegetation made Lottie feel claustrophobic and vulnerable. "I know there are houses on either side but I don't like the thought of being tucked away unable to see the road especially knowing there's a burglar on the loose."

"And a murderer or two."

"Yes, of course."

"I agree though. I shouldn't like to be hidden like that but hopefully on Friday she'll be able to look from her windows and watch the world go by as we're doing now."

Only Sandra was home when they reached the Old Bakehouse. Bill and Zac were at work and the girls at school.

"When do they break up?" Lottie asked as they took seats in the sitting room.

"In a couple of weeks. So at the moment I'm making the most of every day and enjoying the peace and quiet when I'm not at work."

"I don't blame you."

"Would you like tea?"

"Only if you're having one," said Hetty.

Sandra laughed. "I drink gallons of tea. Our kettle hardly ever has the chance to cool down."

When the tea was made and Sandra was seated she looked at the sisters in an agitated manner. "I'm glad you've called today because I want to ask your advice. It's about Zac and Emma. They've applied for a house on the new estate and want to move in together. One of those for rent, you know, for local people." Her voice trembled as she spoke.

Hetty was very positive. "I think it's a lovely idea, Sandra, I really do. They're clearly made for each other and the houses are in a lovely location. Lottie and I popped up to see how they're coming along only the other day."

"Yes, yes, I appreciate that the houses are nice and all that but don't you think they're too young?" Sandra's hands shook as she attempted to sip her tea. "Don't get me wrong. I want them both to be happy and when Zac told us it was obvious he's very keen on the idea but I just think it's too soon and they should wait a few more years."

Lottie was reluctant to take sides. "What does Bill think?"

"He thinks it's a good idea. He said a chap needs to stand on his own two feet and go out into the big wide world. He also said it will do Zac good. Make a man of him and all that."

Lottie tutted. "Typical Bill."

"But he does have a point," said Hetty, "and were they lucky enough to get a house they'd not be far away. Some parents see their children travel to the other side of the world so I'd not be too upset if I were you, Sandra."

Lottie half-smiled. "And don't forget your sister-in-law is living in the States. It was very hard for Hugh and me when she went and I still miss her."

Sandra bit her bottom lip. "Of course, I'm sorry. I'd forgotten about Barbara. We see so little of her and Bill seldom mentions his sister now."

Lottie nodded. "Well, she's happy and that's the main thing."

"Yes she is, and I'm being selfish because you're right about Zac and Emma. I mean, it's not as if they've only just met. They've known each other for three years now even though for much of that time they were three hundred miles apart." Sandra smiled. "And of course, they'd only be renting so if it all went haywire there would be no finances involved and they could leave and go their separate ways. Not that I think they will: as you said they're made for each other."

"So have they actually put their names forward?" Hetty asked.

"Yes, they did it on-line. Houses are allocated on a points system. You know, your rating is higher if you have connections with the village such as work and family. So it's just a matter of waiting now to see if they're lucky or not."

At four o'clock the girls arrived home from school and after greeting their elderly relatives they went up to their rooms with drinks and snacks. Half an hour later, Zac returned home from work.

"Are you and Sid still working in the pub?" Hetty asked.

"No, we finished there some time ago. All the tradesmen have finished and gone now: after all, the pub opens again on Friday."

"Of course. Silly me. My mouth opened before my brain had a chance to get in gear."

Zac sat down with a mug of coffee. "I expect you've heard the latest news."

"About your potential move, yes." Hetty smiled approvingly, "I think it's a lovely idea and I shall keep my fingers crossed for you both."

"No, no, I wasn't referring to that but thank you all the same."

"What then?" Sandra asked.

"About Miranda Snow."

Hetty gasped. "Good heavens, have they found out who drowned her already?"

Zac shook his head. "No, well at least I don't think so. My news is about what she's been up to. You see, rumour has it that she that killed her husband Gavin."

"She did what?" Lottie shouted.

Hetty slapped her hand on her knee. "I knew it. She had guilt written all over her face."

"I'm sure that's not right, Zac," gushed Lottie, "someone must have their wires crossed. I remember being told that Sophie Shepherd said the poor woman was in a terrible state when she first saw her the day after she arrived here. Apparently she sat on the bus stop bench in floods of tears and was inconsolable."

"Crocodile tears," scoffed Hetty, "or if they were genuine it was because she was suddenly overcome with guilt. Anyway, we've seen her a couple of times since then and neither time did she look or act grief stricken."

Sandra frowned. "And even if what you say is right, Zac, who can have killed Miranda and why?"

"I don't know about that. I only know that she killed Gavin. At least that's what's being said and it makes sense if you think about it."

"Does it?" Sandra clearly thought not.

"But I don't see how she could have done it if she was in London shopping." Lottie dreaded her sister having guessed right and knew if that were the case she'd never hear the end of it.

"Ah, but that's because she wasn't in London, she was right here in Pentrillick." The three ladies looked nonplussed. Zac put down his coffee mug. "Let me explain."

Lottie nodded. "Yes, please do because I'm very confused."

"Well, apparently, Miranda had a friend in Bodmin called Patty. They've known each other since they were at school and are, were, best mates. I don't know why, greed I suppose, but the two of them decided that if they could get rid of Gavin then Miranda would get a large sum of money from his life insurance policy. The problem was that if Miranda disposed of him, she, being his closest family member and the one to benefit from the pay-out would be questioned by the police and so she would need a rock solid alibi."

"Which she apparently had," interrupted Lottie.

Zac shook his head. "Ah, but she didn't. You see, it turns out that it wasn't Miranda who went to London at all, it was Patty. They booked the hotel room in Miranda's name and then

113

Patty went up there wearing Miranda's clothes and a wig in the same style and colour as Miranda's hair. They wanted to be sure that, if the police checked CCTV, Patty could easily be mistaken for Miranda. Patty purposely kept her train ticket too so that Miranda could show it to the police. The ticket of course had been paid for with her own debit card. Miranda also had clothes, shoes and other things bought by Patty in London but using Miranda's card. They even swapped cars so that Patty could leave Miranda's car at the station and Patty took Miranda's mobile with her in case they checked it for location and stuff like that."

"Cunning so-and-sos," spluttered Hetty, "Were it not so ghastly I'd be impressed."

Zac picked up his coffee mug. "That's just what Sid said."

"Meanwhile, I suppose Miranda came down here in Patty's car and lurked around waiting for the opportunity to kill poor old Gavin," said Sandra.

"That's right and she took her chance when she saw him leaving the hotel after several pints. She then ran ahead and waited in the churchyard."

"I'm really shocked," admitted Hetty, "even though I knew it was her I didn't expect it would have been so perfectly planned."

"But how did they end up in the churchyard?" Lottie still hoped the gossip was wrong, "I know Gavin was thin but Miranda wouldn't have be able to drag him in there especially as there are a couple of steps."

"Apparently she waited for him in the churchyard and when she saw him approaching she called his name. I suppose he went in there to see who had called out of curiosity."

"And en route she must have grabbed Bill's hanging basket," tutted Lottie.

"Yeah, poor Dad. Apparently the original plan was to hit him over the head with a stone or an urn off one of the graves as they knew there would be something suitable, but when she saw the basket she thought that was a much better weapon. And before you ask, they knew the layout of the village because they'd studied it on Google Street View. They also knew he'd be alone because there was a match on and he hated football. This was established when he went home the previous weekend. He told her then about the match and said he'd have to go out and leave his mates to watch it."

"But if this is all true how on earth did the police find out it out?" Sandra asked.

Zac drained his coffee mug and reached across to the fruit bowl for a banana. "Patty was questioned by the police after Miranda's body was found because she was the last person that Miranda had spoken to on the phone. When she learned her friend was dead she broke down and eventually confessed."

"And I suppose it was Patty that Miranda met up with for the boozy night out," reasoned Hetty.

Sandra shook her head. "No, what you've said, Zac, can't be right surely because the police would never have released those details. It would be most unethical. So someone must be telling their own theory as fact."

"But it is true, Mum. You see, before Patty confessed to the police she told her sister what they'd done because she wanted her sister and the family to hear it from her rather than read about it in the papers. Her sister who is younger, has a boyfriend who works for S. P. Roach & Son and when the boyfriend heard he told his fellow workers and they told Sid."

"But the tradesmen have all gone home," Lottie was confused, "So how can they have told Sid?"

"You're right, they have gone home. But thinking it was only right that people down here knew what had happened, Vince rang Sid last night and told him all about it and of course Sid told me."

"Dear oh dear. Money certainly is the root of all evil," tutted Lottie.

Hetty nodded. "Yes, and because of her greed Patty has lost a friend and her freedom. Silly, silly girl."

Sandra shook her head in disbelief. "And the only one to benefit is the insurance company."

Chapter Seventeen

"So, let me get this right," said Debbie, as she and her friends sat around a table in the village hall later that evening ready to play bingo. "Miranda killed her husband to get the insurance money by swapping places with a friend and so forth. I can understand that. Well, not understand why she did it but I can understand what you're saying. What I'm baffled by though is who on earth then could have killed her and why? Because when I heard Miranda's death wasn't suicide I assumed the same person was responsible for both crimes. Them being married and so forth."

"Exactly," Hetty agreed, "we thought the same. Now we're at a loss as to what happened."

"Well, what with that and the burglaries we certainly have plenty of things to occupy our time for the rest of this summer." Debbie was in a state of shock.

"I reckon it must have been someone close to Gavin, a best friend maybe, and he killed Miranda to get justice." Lottie spoke quietly as a couple of women took seats on the next table.

"In which case he must have known that she was guilty," reasoned Debbie.

"Good point," Hetty agreed, "and it might not even have been a male friend. It could have been an ex-girlfriend of Gavin's."

"Or a current one," whispered Lottie.

"I'm sure it would have been a man as it'd take some strength to push someone under the water and hold them there 'til they drowned." Debbie shuddered at the thought.

Lottie nodded. "Yes and despite what I said about a girlfriend, I think I have to agree."

"Me too," said Hetty, "but whoever did it, it was obviously premeditated because it's reckoned the chap or girl went into her room through the window."

"But I thought it's said her room was on the second floor." Debbie scowled.

"It was."

"In that case it has to be an inside job. You know someone with access to a master key card or something like that."

Hetty removed her cardigan and hung it on the back of her chair. "Sounds feasible but we heard from Norman that the police definitely think he got in through the window. It was slightly open, you see and Norman reported his suspicion that there was someone outside the hotel the night before she died who was behaving in a furtive manner. When he called out and asked if there was anyone there, no-one answered which is hardly surprising, is it? Anyway, he's even convinced he saw a shadow but then he might not have as he'd had a few pints that night and being midnight he was probably tired."

Lottie nodded. "Yes, and the imagination is inclined to play tricks on the mind when one is feeling sleepy. What's more, remember we'd been telling ghost stories earlier that evening so that might have spooked him too."

"Well if someone got in through her window he must have been a rock climber or a mountaineer," whispered Debbie, convinced the women on the neighbouring table were eavesdropping, "because no ordinary person could climb that wall."

"He might have had a ladder," suggested Lottie, "be easy then as long as he had a head for heights."

Hetty laughed. "I think he might have been spotted if he'd walked through the village carrying a ladder."

"Not if he's a window cleaner," reasoned Debbie, "or even a builder."

Hetty took her reading glasses from her handbag ready to play bingo. "Well whatever, I think a few glasses of wine are in order after tonight's games, then we can watch the hotel staff and see if any of them look suspicious."

"But we know most of the staff already," laughed Lottie, "so there will be nothing to learn there."

"Ah, but we've never viewed them as suspects before, have we? Anyway, it might not be one of the staff. The killer could be one of the guests."

When they arrived at the hotel they were surprised to find Tess Dobson behind the bar. The three ladies promptly headed in her direction.

"Hey, lovely to see you but what are you doing here?" Hetty asked.

"Just helping out for a few days because a couple of the staff are off sick."

"That's nice. Nice that you're able to help, I mean, and not nice that they're off sick." Hetty hoped her babbled words made sense.

"We've missed seeing you with the pub being closed," said Lottie, "and there's not much chance to natter at the Gardening Club meetings."

"I've missed being there too. The tea shop's a nice place to work but it's not the same as the pub." Debbie straightened a beer mat on the bar.

"Yes, no gossip I should imagine."

"Very little."

"So will you be going back to the pub with the new folks when it opens?" Lottie asked.

"Yes, James actually approached me and said there was a job for me if I wanted and with as many hours as I like. I think Ashley and Alison had put in a good word for me. Bless them. Anyway, are you ladies wanting a drink?"

"Yes, please, Tess. Three glasses of merlot." Hetty took her purse from her handbag.

"Large?"

"Need you ask?"

Tess laughed as she reached for three glasses.

"So out of curiosity, when did you start here?" Debbie asked.

"On Saturday evening."

"Damn! That's a shame. I was hoping you were going to say last week so you would have been here when Miranda Snow died, even though we know you weren't here the night before because we were, if that makes sense."

"I wish I had been. The pathologist reckon she died around nine o'clockish so the bar would have been open then."

"We think it might have been an inside job," whispered Debbie, "you know, one of the staff with access to a master key card or something like that."

Tess shook her head. "No nothing that simple. The hotel has CCTV and I can assure you that the police have been through it rigorously and no-one entered her room by the door until the chambermaid went in the next morning."

Lottie gasped. "Oh no, poor chambermaid, that must have been a nasty shock for her."

"It was. She's one of the people off sick. She did a couple of days after but couldn't cope. She's hoping to be back at the weekend but she won't be chambermaiding anymore. The boss is going to get her trained up for reception."

"How about outside?" Lottie was deep in thought.

Tess laughed. "Outside what?"

"Oh, sorry. I'm thinking CCTV cameras. Are there any outside near Miranda's window?"

"Sadly not. There's one on the front entrance and another round the back but nothing looking at the building itself."

Hetty paid for the drinks with her bank debit card. "So, was anyone seen coming in through the main entrance?"

"No, so it's assumed whoever he was climbed over the wall and came in through the shrubbery at the side."

"Interesting," Lottie drummed her fingers on the bar, "because that's where Norman thought he saw someone on the Tuesday night so I bet whoever he was had been sussing it out and hid a ladder amongst the shrubs either that night or sometime on Wednesday."

Hetty placed her bank card back in her purse. "Couldn't have been the night before. Remember, Norman said on Wednesday morning that he checked for signs of anyone having been there on his way out to buy flowers and I'm sure he would have spotted a ladder."

Once the ladies were seated at their usual table they began to mull over information received and just as Lottie was about to comment on access to Miranda's room, Clara Bragg emerged from the dining room with the man they had seen her with before.

"Well, he can't be a journalist because he wouldn't interview her twice." Debbie was the first to see them as she was facing the dining room door.

Hetty frowned. "Who wouldn't interview who twice?"

"The good looking man and Clara." Debbie nodded towards the couple as they took seats on the opposite side of the bar, "It looks like he's been in the sun too because he's definitely a shade darker than the last time we saw him."

Lottie glanced over her shoulder. "I wonder who he is then."

"It's just a thought," reflected Debbie, "but do you think he might be Pentrillick's mysterious burglar?"

Lottie gasped. "Good point, he might well be."

"Don't be daft," chuckled Hetty, "he doesn't look a bit like Jason King and if he did he'd hardly come in here right under everyone's noses."

Debbie thoughtfully twisted a strand of hair around her finger. "I don't know, it's reckoned that bad guys often hide out near to their crime scenes. And who said the burglar looks like Jason King?"

"It was me" Hetty confessed, "when the police officer described him that's who came to mind. I was feeling rather frivolous at the time but then that's another story."

"I suppose it still might be him," reasoned Lottie, "I mean the curly hair that Elliot Harris saw could well have been a wig and the moustache could have been false."

"Good point," Hetty glanced to where Clara sat with the mystery man, "I wonder if he has a tattoo on the back of his hand."

Lottie shrugged her shoulders. "Well even if he doesn't have one it could still be him because you can put on temporary tattoos these days."

A frown crossed Debbie's face as she listened to the sisters. "Okay, I give up. Who is Elliot Harris?"

Hetty tutted. "Keep up, Debbie. He's the taxi driver who lives in Honeysuckle Drive and who disturbed the burglar when he got home."

"From a barbecue in Penzance," Lottie added.

"Oh, yes of course. I'm not very good at remembering names but he's the lovely chap who drove Gideon and me to Marazion and back and who sings out of tune."

Lottie nodded. "Spot on."

The unknown man suddenly stood up; all three ladies watched as he left Clara at the table and went to the bar for drinks.

"Quick, quick, drink up, ladies, I'm going to go up for refills while he's still there." Hetty quickly drained her own glass and stood up.

"Surely you're not going to ask him who he is," Lottie was aghast.

"No, of course not. I just want to hear if he says anything that might give us a clue as to who he might be and so forth."

"But you paid for the last round, it's my turn now." Debbie quickly grabbed a twenty pound note from her purse and thrust it in Hetty's hand, "Here take this."

"Thank you," Hetty picked up the three empty glasses and hurried over to the bar. After the stranger had been served, she asked for the same again.

"So, umm, who's the chap with Clara? Any idea, Tess?"

"Oh, that's Steve. He's staying here. Nice chap."

"He's staying here. So how come he knows Clara?"

"No idea but they've met in here on several occasions."

"Any idea where he's from?"

Tess removed the cork from a new bottle of merlot. "Not exactly, but he has a Liverpool accent and I believe he's in insurance. Something like that anyway."

"Really! Any idea of his surname?"

"Frost. His name is Steve Frost."

"Frost! As in the same as Miranda?" Hetty put her hand over her mouth and hoped Steve had not heard her raised voice.

Tess laughed. "No, silly. She wasn't Frost: she was Snow."

"Ah, I'm one up on you there, Tess," Hetty looked over her shoulder and lowered her voice, "Snow was Miranda's married name but her maiden name was Frost."

Tess stopped pouring the wine. "Are you sure, Het?"

"Absolutely, we got it from Sid who got it from either Vince, Leo or Matt."

"Max," corrected Tess, "it's Max who works with Leo and Vince."

"Yes, you're right," Hetty was about to ask more questions but stopped when someone else approached the bar. Instead she picked up the refilled glasses, thanked Tess and returned to Debbie and Lottie.

Chapter Eighteen

On Thursday morning, the sisters walked down to the village with a few items they no longer wanted - their destination: the charity shop. They reached the bottom of Long Lane just as a police car drove by.

"Oh dear. I hope that doesn't mean another crime has been committed." Hetty watched as the car disappeared around the corner.

"Likewise, but if there has been let's hope it's a burglary and not another murder."

"I couldn't agree more and what would be really nice is to hear that the police have just come from the hotel because there have been some developments but I think it's unlikely."

"We can but hope you're right but I think it's more likely that they're just passing through. After all they didn't have the blue lights flashing or the sirens on."

"True, but then they wouldn't anyway unless they were going towards an emergency of some sort."

"On the other hand, they're probably just keeping an eye out for the Jason King lookalike."

Hetty chuckled. "That's a point. I wonder if they've had any luck with that."

Lottie stopped walking. "It's only just struck me, Het, but do you think there might be a connection between the burglaries and the two murders?"

"There might be but I think it's unlikely. I mean, what possible connection could there be?"

"No idea. It was just a thought and I suppose I'm trying to minimalise the number of criminals in our midst and the burglaries did start around the same time that Gavin was throttled." Lottie took a few quick steps to catch up with her sister.

"Yes, but Miranda killed Gavin. We know that so I don't see any connection at all."

After passing over their donations to Maisie, Hetty commented on the police car.

Daisy laughed. "Nothing much slips past you two, does it?"

"Not if we can help it." Hetty was too thick skinned to notice the jibe.

"Actually they had been here," admitted Maisie, "We called them you see when we heard about the rope."

Hetty frowned. "Rope. I don't understand."

"I'll put the kettle on." Daisy slipped into a small back room.

Maisie leaned her elbows on the shop's counter. "We had a long piece of thick rope stolen from the shop a week or so ago. We wouldn't have noticed but Bernie the Boatman came in this morning because Veronica had seen it a while back and she thought it might be useful for his boat. Needless to say, she didn't buy it at the time when she first saw it because he might not have needed it, if you see what I mean. Anyway, he forgot all about it until Veronica reminded him last night and so he came in this morning to see if we still had it. We said we had but when we went to get it we found it had gone. Neither of us had sold it though and so we assumed it'd been stolen. That's why we phoned the police."

"Clear as mud," scoffed Hetty.

Lottie nodded her agreement.

Maisie raised her eyebrows. "It does make sense, honest. You see, someone was in here the other day saying that the police reckoned the murderer got in through Miranda Snow's hotel window and so we figured that he would have needed a rope or a ladder to climb the wall."

"Yes, I suppose so," Hetty hoped she didn't look as confused as she felt.

Lottie was quicker off the mark. "Are you implying the rope that was stolen from here was used by the murderer to access Miranda's room?"

"Yes, possibly but that's for the police to find out."

"Find out who took it you mean?" quizzed Lottie.

Daisy returned with a pot of tea and four mugs on a tray. "Yes, but they've got their work cut out because we weren't much help as we've no idea who might have taken it. It's really frustrating. We don't even know on which day it went missing."

"I can see now what you're implying, but who's to say the rope is the same one," reasoned Lottie, "I mean, how on earth would they be able to tell?"

"I don't know but the police reckon it was. It was thick and a good length," stated Maisie.

"And really strong," Daisy passed a mug of tea to Hetty.

"Thank you, but I'm still confused. I mean, if a rope was used it would have needed something on the wall to get attached to, so what might that have been?"

"Apparently there's a wooden trellis running from the ground, up the wall and alongside Miranda's window. It's secured at the top beside the lintel by two large metal pegs and it's assumed they were used for the rope's attachment," divulged Maisie.

Daisy handed a mug of tea to Lottie. "Yes, and we were just saying before you arrived that whoever he is must be pretty good at lassoing to have got it up there. Although after several attempts he might just have got lucky."

"Okay, I'll accept all that but why then would someone risk stealing a rope in the first place when he could quite simply have come in and bought it?" Lottie placed her mug of tea on a stack of plates.

Daisy shook her head. "Because we might have remembered him, I suppose."

"I assume you don't have CCTV which is a pity." Lottie cast her eyes around the shop in search of a camera.

"That's what we said but we don't and it wouldn't be worth it anyway," said Maisie. "As we often say if someone steals from a charity shop they must be pretty desperate."

"Or in this case, a murderer," Hetty added.

As Zac finished work on Thursday afternoon his phone rang; it was Emma who told him that she had been advised by someone in the know that if she and Zac were to be successful and offered a house it would be useful for them to have some preference as to which house they might be interested in. Zac, who was familiar with the estate and its layout suggested they go along there one evening and take a quick look around for although Emma had seen the plans online and had printed details too, she said it was difficult to make a choice from computer generated pictures and room dimensions. As neither Zac nor Emma had anything planned for that evening they decided that there was no time like the present. Consequently, just after six, Emma called for Zac and they made their way through the village and up the lane leading to the new estate. However, they told no-one where they were going or why as the estate, being a building site was not open to unauthorised visitors.

On arrival, they climbed over a wall at the side rather than open the temporary gate which stretched across the site entrance. Zac then pointed out the ten houses to be rented, all were semi-detached; two had four bedrooms, six had three bedrooms and two had two bedrooms. To enable them to see the kitchens they went around the back of the houses, climbed over heaps of rubble and systematically peeped in the downstairs windows of each one.

"What do you think?" Zac asked, as they sat down on up-turned wheelbarrows.

"Well, it's obvious that as there are just the two of us we would only be eligible for a two bedroomed house which actually is rather fortuitous because my favourite is number seven."

"I knew you'd like that one and it just so happens it's my favourite too. I know the kitchen units aren't in yet but you can still sense what it will be like and being west facing means it'll be nice and sunny for when we get home from work."

As they sat and talked of their dreams and aspirations a sudden noise caused them to sit up straight. "What was that?" Emma whispered.

"I'm not sure but it sounded a bit like the clatter of the entrance gates closing," Zac reached over and took Emma's hand, "let's move around the corner where we'll be less conspicuous."

Crouched behind a block of portable toilets they heard voices.

"It sounds like someone is around the front of the houses," said Zac.

The voices grew quieter.

Emma stood up. "It's probably someone doing the same as us."

Zac stood too. "It does but whoever they are they've gone past here and down towards the houses that are for sale."

"Let's follow them."

"But they might see us."

"Doesn't matter if they do because they shouldn't be here anymore than us."

"True. Come on then."

Holding hands they crept along the road to the furthest side of the site and as they reached the detached houses for sale on the open market they saw two people disappear around the back of the one on the end.

"Did you recognise either of them?"

Zac shook his head. "No, did you?"

"No."

Intrigued they walked up to the neighbouring house and from its back garden area watched from behind a newly erected fence. To their surprise the couple seemed to have no interest in the house. A woman carried an old washing up bowl beneath her arm in which were several sickly flowering plants; in her free hand she carried a trowel. A man followed her as she approached the boundary wall of the care home.

"You wait here," they heard her say.

With bowl in hand she disappeared over the wall and into dense shrubbery; ten minutes later she returned with the bowl brim-full of healthy plants and gone were their sickly relations.

"Why couldn't you have got them from the garden centre? It would have been much easier."

"Because it's too late to get summer bedding plants now you numpty and these gazanias are stunning and far better than mine ever looked."

"But surely someone will notice that you've swapped them over."

"No they won't. Residents rarely come up this far and even if they did they'd just think the slugs had been having a feast." She turned towards the house, "Come on, let's go as I want to get these in my tubs tonight before they wilt."

"Okay, Clara, but don't take too long because I want to get back to the hotel for dinner. I did quite a bit of swimming today and I'm starving."

Zac quietly chuckled. "Clara. She has to be Clara Bragg then. Wait 'til I tell Mum and Dad, it'll have them in fits."

"But that means you'll have to tell them we were up here."

"Yes, it will, but it'll be worth it just to see their faces."

That same evening, Kate and Vicki went to work in the pub where they had part-time jobs for the summer season. It was their first evening with the new licensees and all staff were working to get ready for the grand opening the following evening.

"How did you get on?" Bill switched off the television set when his daughters arrived home.

"Alright," said Kate, "James and Ella are nice but they seemed a bit anxious. I think I preferred Alison and Ashley."

"I'm not surprised they're anxious. I would be too if I'd spent the money they must have getting the pub extended and so forth. And they're no doubt a bit nervous about opening for the first time tomorrow and meeting all the locals."

"Yeah, you could be right. The pub looks great anyway and the new loos are gorgeous. Both Ladies and Gents have a shower room and separate loos attached for campers to use and there are doors for access from outside as well as from the bar, but of course the doors between the bar and the loos will be locked when the pub's closed."

"They've thought of everything," said Bill.

"They have and you should see the pictures painted by Ella, they're brill. I wish I could paint like that." Vicki dropped a carrier bag onto the floor and then flopped down on the sofa beside her sister.

"What's in the bag?" Bill asked.

"White polo shirts," Vicki picked up the bag, tipped its contents onto her lap and held up one of the shirts. "See they have Crown and Anchor embroidered on the pockets. All the staff are going to wear them."

"James and Ella aren't," corrected Kate, "they'll be all dressed up. I think they're just for us waitresses and kitchen staff."

Bill watched as Vicki attempted to fold the shirts, gave up and then bundled them into the bag. "So who else was there this evening?"

Kate counted on her fingers. "Tess Dobson, she'll be on the bar tomorrow with James and Ella and then in the kitchen it was us and two other girls who we didn't know but they're really, really nice. James and Ella also have a son too who'll help on the bar. Tess told us he's been away on holiday since he broke up from university and only arrived in Cornwall today and it was the first time he'd seen the pub. Tess met him when she got there but he'd gone out by the time we arrived."

"Or perhaps he was in his room," reasoned Vicki.

"Yeah, could have been, I suppose. Anyway, whatever, we didn't see him."

"What about the chef?" asked Bill, "you haven't mentioned him yet. I assume he was there."

Kate plumped up the cushion behind her back "Oh, no I haven't. Silly me of course he was there."

"So what's he like?"

"Smashing, isn't he, Vicki? He's funny too and kept making us girls laugh. We've been helping him prepare food for the opening and he said he'll teach us how to cook *real* Italian food."

"He'll be ordering large sacks of pasta then," said Bill.

"What! Don't be daft, Dad, he's the real deal and makes his own," scoffed Vicki.

"Oh. So is he renting a house somewhere or is he living in the pub?"

Vicki shook her head. "He was in the pub but he's moved into one of the caravans that the builders were in now. James said he's going to just keep the one and then sell the others to make more room for anyone wanting to camp on the field."

"And I think Benvolio's caravan is only a temporary thing," Kate added, "because he said he'd like to buy one of the new houses when they're ready and then his mum can come and live here too."

"Whose mum is coming to live here?" Sandra had been upstairs changing ready to do the night shift at the care home.

"The new chef's mum," said Bill.

"Oh, that's nice," Sandra reached under the chair for her comfy shoes, "I know Italians are very family orientated."

"Does he have any other family?" Bill asked.

Kate shrugged her shoulders. "No idea. He didn't say and we didn't ask."

"He says he doesn't have a girlfriend," giggled Vicki, "we know that because Tess asked him and he laughed and said no, but there was definitely a twinkle in his eyes, so actually he might have one and he's keeping her a secret."

Sandra picked up her handbag and checked to make sure that she had her keys. "She's probably up-country somewhere so you'd be none the wiser if he'd named her."

"That's true," acknowledged Vicki, "and maybe he's not saying much because she might not want to come and live down here, especially if she has a good job up-country."

Kate took off her shoes and tucked her feet snuggly by her side. "Well, whatever the reason, I think he does have a girlfriend and that her name is Sophia because he has that name tattooed on his arm, doesn't he, Vicki?"

"Yes, in a big heart with flowers."

"Ah, so she has the same name as Ivor's missus," reflected Bill.

"No, Dad. Ivor's wife is Sophie."

"It's an easy mistake to make, Kate, as Ivor often calls his wife Soph." Sandra left the room to collect her jacket from the hallway.

"Bill stood to kiss her goodbye when she returned. "Did you know that James and Ella have a son, Sandra?"

"No, I didn't. Have you girls met him then?"

Kate shook her head. "No, but we'll see him tomorrow."

"And hopefully he'll be gorgeous," Vicki added.

"Now that would be too much to ask. I reckon he'll either be goofy or a geek."

Chapter Nineteen

"Thank goodness the pub's opening up again tonight," cheered Hetty, as she and Lottie ate breakfast on Friday morning. "Having the chance to meet up with and chat to more people means we might get a better insight as to what's been happening over the last few weeks."

Lottie laughed. "Maybe, although I don't think seeing everyone will help in any way to solve the current crimes. But it'll certainly be lovely to go there again and I'm really looking forward to seeing what James and Ella have had done to the place."

"Me too and I suggest we get there early as the bar is likely to be packed."

"Yes, but before that there is work to be done, Het."

"There certainly is and I've a feeling today is going to be very productive in more ways than one."

In the afternoon, the six members of the Gardening Club who had volunteered assembled outside Sunnyside, the bungalow with overgrown gardens near to Sea View Cottage. Once everyone had arrived they informed Betsy Triggs, the owner, they were there and then began their work. Sally, Tommy and Tess, set to clearing brambles, ivy, nettles and convolvulus that engulfed a shrubbery at the front of the building; at the same time on the other side of the path, Bill, Sandra and Clara cut through the two foot high grass and weeds hoping to restore the area to its original form as a lawn.

It was warm work and the volunteers were grateful for the dappled shade provided by a large cherry tree.

Betsy Triggs who seldom left the house was delighted to receive the help and had offered members the use of her kitchen to make tea and coffee. To show her appreciation she had also ordered cakes to be delivered from the local shop and pasties to arrive at one o'clock for the workers' lunches. While the work was in progress outside, Hetty and Lottie, who had volunteered to look after the catering side for the day, made the tea and coffee and chatted to the elderly widow in the comfort of her sitting room between tea breaks.

"I had a bit of fun here last night," a broad smile crossed Betsy's face and her eyes twinkled. Neither sister was sure they wanted to know what the fun might be. "I had the police here, you see. They were hidden mind you."

"Police? Why were they here?" Hetty instinctively glanced over her shoulder.

"Because I'd called them."

Lottie was intrigued. "We're all ears."

Seeing she had the full attention of the sisters, Betsy leaned forwards and rested her hands on her knees. "I'll tell you why I called them, and it's like this. A couple of days ago I had a visit from a young man saying that he was doing surveys in the village and my instincts told me that he was up to no good. You see, like everyone else I'd had a visit from the police who told me that there was a burglar in the area and they asked if I'd seen anyone behaving in a suspicious manner. At that time I hadn't but as I've already said, this survey man raised my suspicions. Anyway, I invited him in and did his survey; when he asked about hobbies and so forth I thought I'd test him out so I told him that I didn't get out much except on Thursdays when I always go and stay with a friend overnight."

"Oh, that's nice," said Lottie.

Betsy chuckled. "Well it would be if it were true but I made it up. You see, I reckoned if I told him that and he was the burglar then he'd come back and break in on Thursday while I was supposedly away. I knew I'd roused his interest because after that he kept fidgeting and craning his neck to look round the room, like he was casing the joint as they say. Needless to say as soon as he had gone I phoned the police and they came straight round. I don't think they were really convinced by what I told them and I'm even prepared to admit they were probably humouring me but nevertheless they came up with a plan where they'd be here last night waiting for him just in case I was right. Of course they wanted me to be out of the house but I said no, not on your nelly, I'm not missing this. So they let me stay but I had to be in my bedroom with the lights off. They of course waited in here. It was so exciting."

Lottie was on the edge of her seat. "And did he turn up?"

"You bet. He was here just after midnight. I heard glass break and reckoned it was the kitchen window. I then heard footsteps on the floorboards in the hallway. Next thing I knew there was a commotion. They caught him red-handed as he dropped my silver candlesticks into a rucksack."

"You were very brave," Hetty was utterly astonished, "I'm not sure that I would have done that."

Lottie laughed. "Yes, you would, Het."

"Yes, I suppose I might have. So, Betsy, did he fit the description given by the police? You know, a white male, early to mid-thirties, five foot tennish, medium build, a tattoo on the back of his hand, and what was the other thing, Lottie?"

"Thick curly dark brown hair and a droopy moustache."

"Yes, of course. Silly me. The biggest giveaways of all."

Betsy shook her head. "Yes and no. He was the right age, build and colour but as for hair, he had none and likewise no moustache or tattoo...."

"Oh," Hetty was both surprised and disappointed.

"And there's a very good reason for that. You see, after I heard about the attempted robbery that was thwarted when someone or other came home early, I immediately smelt a rat. The description was too good for someone claiming to have just caught a glimpse of the burglar as he escaped through the window and for that reason I took his account of the so called attempted robbery with a pinch of salt."

"My goodness. Are you saying that Elliot Harris, the taxi driver from Honeysuckle Drive told a few porkies?" Lottie was taken aback.

"Yes, and that's because *he* is the burglar so not only did he tell a few porkies, he made the whole thing up to throw the police and everyone else off the right track."

Hetty's jaw dropped. "But if you were in your bedroom, how do you know that it was Elliot Harris who was caught red-handed?"

"Because when I heard the commotion I crept out of my bedroom and peeped in here. The police were too busy to notice." She chuckled, "It was just like the cop programmes on the telly and I was in time to hear a police officer say that he recognised the burglar having met him before at his house in Honeysuckle Drive. The policeman then said in a very serious voice, 'Elliot Harris, you are under arrest on suspicion of burglary. You do not have to say anything, but it may harm your defence if you do not mention when questioned something which you later rely on in court.' There was more to it than that but I can't remember the exact words even though I've heard them umpteen times on television police dramas. Whatever though it was really exciting. Having said that Elliot didn't look very happy and after he was taken away in hand-cuffs I felt sorry for him. I mean, he probably wasn't a bad person, but just struggling to make ends meet and he told me when we did the survey that he was really looking forward to the pub opening because it had closed before he came to the village and so he'd never been inside. And now the police have him so he'll miss it and he was ever so nice, poor chap."

"You're too soft, Betsy." Lottie reached out and patted the elderly lady's arm.

"I never used to be. It was my late husband who changed my way of thinking. He was a good man and saw no bad in anyone."

"Well, no wonder the burglar was never seen by anyone," tutted Lottie, "if the description given was false."

Hetty tutted. "Shame though because I was looking forward to seeing a Jason King lookalike."

Lottie laughed. "Trust you, Het. As for you, Betsy, I have to confess that I'm full of admiration for your bravery."

"And your perspicacity too," Hetty added.

Betsy rose from the sofa and took a photograph from the wall in an alcove by the fireplace. "This is me many, many years ago when I was in the WRAF. I may look frail now but I can assure you back then I was as tough as old boots. What's more, I have a good brain and I worked in Intelligence."

"Wow, I'm impressed," admitted Lottie.

"Me too," Hetty folded her arms, "So out of curiosity, Betsy, have you any idea who murdered Miranda Snow? We've been trying to fathom it out but seem to be getting nowhere?"

Betsy shook her head. "Sadly I can't help you there as I've never had any contact with the people involved. Never even seen them in fact."

By the time the group working outside stopped for their lunch break the garden already looked much improved. A hydrangea, strangled by convolvulus bounced back into shape as the twisted strands of the weed were cut from its branches and by the boundary wall which separated the garden from the house next door, a fuchsia seemed to relish its freedom from the choking ivy.

For their lunch break, Betsy insisted they all sit in her sitting room rather than outside where there were no chairs and, to entertain them as they ate their pasties, Hetty suggested that she repeat the events of the previous evening which she was more than happy to do. No-one spoke as they listened in awe to the elderly lady's yarn and all congratulated her on giving them peace of mind knowing the burglar was at last under arrest.

After an hour's relaxation, the volunteers went back outside to continue their work; on the side of the path where the grass had been cut back, they began to tackle a rampant escallonia hedge. Bill, on a step ladder cut back the top with an electric hedge trimmer, while Sandra and Clara tackled either side of the hedge with garden shears. As the hedge was reduced to a manageable size, Clara, who was working out on the pavement, spotted a carrier bag tucked between the wall and the hedge. Intrigued as to what it might contain, she pulled it from its hiding place and took it into the garden.

"What have you got there?" Bill switched off the hedge trimmer.

"I'm just about to find out." Clara turned the bag upside-down and tipped its contents onto the path. From it fell a black jacket with wet sleeves, a pair of black leather gloves and a black balaclava.

Having finished creating the new garden of the Crown and Anchor earlier in the week, the gardeners from Pentrillick House who had worked on the project were back doing their normal chores and duties. Down by the lake, Debbie's husband, Gideon laboured with Robert Oliver tidying the woodland path and putting down fresh bark.

"Have your wife and her friends been back for another game of bowls?" Robert asked. "Sally said they were very good for beginners."

Gideon stopped and leaned on his rake. "I don't think they've got time at the moment. They're too busy trying to solve the mystery of Miranda Snow's murder."

Robert laughed. "You're pulling my leg. I mean, surely people only do that in story books."

Gideon shook his head. "You've clearly not met my wife and her friends."

"Well actually I have. Remember you introduced me to them at the Gardening Club's first meeting, although I don't think I've had cause to say more than a few words to them since then and that was about the Pentrillick in Bloom competition."

"Well, I can assure you, hand on heart, that they really are having a go. Whether or not they'll come up with the right answer remains to be seen."

"So who do they have in mind? Anyone I know?"

"I've no idea, Robert. I try to keep out of it. All I do know is that at the moment they're keen to find a piece of rope that was stolen from the village charity shop." Gideon laughed. "I should watch out or they'll probably be round to ask you and Sally if you happened to be looking out of your flat window and saw anyone leaving the shop with it."

"It'd be fun if they did, not that we'd be able to help." Robert tipped the remaining bark from the wheelbarrow onto the path and then stopped abruptly. "Hey, I've just remembered something. As I've told you before, Sally goes for a swim every other morning and the other day she got her foot tangled in a piece of rope while in the sea. She didn't know where it'd come from so she put it by the boats on the beach in case it was anything to do with the boat owners."

"Really! Is it still there do you think?"

"No idea. I don't go down to the beach very often. Is the theft of a piece of rope important then?"

"It is if it's what was used by the murderer to climb the wall to get into Miranda Snow's hotel room."

"You're kidding."

"I'm not, really, I'm not."

Robert quickly pulled out his mobile phone. "I'll ring Sally and get her to pass on the information to the police."

Chapter Twenty

When they arrived at the Crown and Anchor a little after six thirty, Hetty and Lottie took a stroll round the pub gardens with Debbie and Gideon to explore before they went inside. Because he had been involved with the landscaping, Gideon took delight in showing them round and naming some of the flowers and shrubs they were unfamiliar with.

"Now that is stunning," Hetty stopped and stood back to admire a kidney shaped flower bed. In its centre on a plinth stood a metal crown and against the plinth leaned a small anchor, "what a novel idea."

Gideon folded his arms. "We thought that. Both were made by a local chap over Truro way somewhere. I think he's done a wonderful job."

"He has," agreed Debbie, "but I hope no-one pinches them."

Gideon shook his head. "They're quite heavy and I can't see why anyone would take them unless it was for scrap metal and that wouldn't be worth the effort."

"I suppose you're right but then if someone else has a pub called the Crown and Anchor they might like them." Hetty pulled her phone from her handbag and took a picture.

Lottie laughed. "Well, it wouldn't take much to track them down then if that were the case, Het."

"Very true."

Lottie turned to Gideon. "Any news yet about the rope?"

Gideon shook his head. "All I know is that Robert asked Sally to report it and she did. They'll probably be in later so we can ask them then."

"Look, Bernie and Veronica are over there." Hetty pointed to where the couple stood, Bernie admiring the new extension and Veronica smelling the jasmine in a tub beside the pub entrance. "If anyone knows about the rope it'll be Bernie." She waved and called them over.

Bernie spoke before anyone had a chance to question him. "I expect you'll be wanting to know why the police were on the beach this afternoon."

Hetty laughed. "We're one up on you there, Bernie, we know why they were there. The question is: did they find the rope?"

"You never miss a trick, do you?"

Gideon explained the conversation he'd had with Robert that afternoon.

"Blimey, I can see what all the fuss was about now then."

"So was the rope still there?" persisted Hetty.

"Yes, it was. It's funny, you know, we'd all seen it but none of us had any idea who it belonged too, although someone suggested it could have been left by some divers who dropped off a motor boat the other day. That seemed a good enough explanation and we thought no more of it."

"Did the police take it away?" Gideon asked.

"Oh yes, and they seemed rather pleased."

"So having seen the rope do you think it might have been used by whoever drowned Miranda as a means to get into her room?" asked Debbie.

Bernie shrugged his shoulders. "Not possible for me to say but I suppose it certainly would have been strong enough and long enough as well."

"And if it is the right rope now all we need to do is find out who pinched it." Hetty rubbed her hands with glee.

Bernie laughed. "Well good luck with that."

As they went inside the pub they were met with music from the nineteen sixties and excited chatter, much of it about Clara's find in the front garden of Sunnyside and the arrest of taxi driver Elliot Harris the night before.

Debbie cast her eyes over the Crown and Anchor's clientèle, all clearly delighted to have their pub open again. "I wish I'd cancelled my dental appointment this afternoon and been here. It must have been really thrilling to be in the village today."

"Oh, it was," enthused Lottie, "my head's spinning with information received and I haven't even had a drink yet."

"It's a shame Clara Bragg found the bag though as I'm sure we'll never hear the end of it," scoffed Hetty.

"Hmm, she did go a bit over the top," agreed Lottie, "and the ear-piercing scream was quite unnecessary. It scared the life out of poor Betsy and sent her cat under the chair."

Debbie looked to where Clara stood telling a small group of her find. "Yes, I can imagine."

Gideon addressed the sisters. "So were you out there when the bag was found?"

Lottie shook her head. "No, we were indoors at the time making tea and coffee with Betsy for the workers' afternoon break."

"Is that when she told you about Elliot's arrest?" Debbie asked.

"No, that was in the morning," Hetty laughed. "Such a shame you weren't there, Debs, because you'd have loved hearing her story and she clearly enjoyed telling it."

Lottie agreed. "She certainly did. You must meet her, Debbie, she's a lovely lady. Hetty and I were so taken with her that we've vowed to call in and see her often so when we go you must come with us."

"Yes, I should like that. It's always nice to meet new people. Am I right in believing she's virtually housebound?"

"Not quite housebound," said Lottie, "She manages to get around and is able to look after herself. You know, she hangs out her washing and stuff like that. She occasionally strolls down to the post office too if the weather's really good. It was her late husband who used to do the garden though and so when he died a couple of years back it started to deteriorate."

On seeing there was a large number of people at the bar waiting to be served Debbie suggested they wait for it to quieten down before buying drinks and in the meantime she asked the sisters to repeat Betsy's tale for Gideon's benefit as in her excitement she may well have missed out some of the finer details told to her by Hetty over the phone earlier.

Lottie smiled as she recalled Betsy's enthusiasm when telling of her escapade. "Shall you tell it, Het, or shall I?"

"You go ahead and I'll be prompter if you forget anything important."

It took a good ten minutes for Lottie to repeat Betsy's story with a little assistance from Hetty which concluded with the widow's sadness on seeing Elliot taken away in handcuffs.

"I don't know: such goings on and I thought the crime rate in Cornwall was supposed to be below the national average," Gideon looked towards the bar where things appeared a little quieter, "Anyway, that's enough chat. Right now I think we all need a drink to celebrate this momentous day. What will you ladies have? My treat."

"That's very kind," said Lottie, "but I think we ought to treat you as you don't very often come out for a drink."

"That's why it's my treat. Anyway, if you want you can do the next round. So what will you have?"

The ladies asked for their usual red wines and while Gideon was at the bar they went to take a quick look in the dining room which they knew had been increased in size as part of the new extension. The door was closed but that didn't deter them, after looking over their shoulders, they crept inside and closed the door behind them. They were impressed by the size, décor, new furniture and in particular the buffet food part-laid out on a long table. As they stood admiring a painting signed by Ella Dale, Kate and Vicki came out with more plates of food. Lottie was taken aback.

"No, I don't believe it. You're dressed the same and now I can't tell you apart."

The girls both giggled.

Hetty looked from one to the other. "Hmm, because you both have your hair in a bun it's not possible to go by the length."

Debbie stepped forward and looked at the twins. After a few minutes she pointed to one of the girls. "This is Vicki," she said, "and so you must be Kate."

Vicki's jaw dropped. "How did you know? No-one else has been able to tell so we've had lots of fun this evening."

"Simple," laughed Debbie, "your nails are longer than Kate's. I've noticed that before. I always look at hands, you see, because for a while many moons ago when I was not much older than you two, I was a manicurist."

As she spoke a tall young man entered the dining room from the bar. He was smartly dressed in black trousers, white shirt and red and silver striped tie; his light brown hair was shaved around the sides and quiffed on the top. When he saw the room was not empty he stopped dead. "Whoops, sorry. I was hoping there would be no-one in here so I could pinch something to eat. I'm starving because Mum's been too busy to think about food."

Kate giggled. "There shouldn't be anyone in here but these ladies are my granny, great aunt and their friend Debbie and as usual they're being nosy."

"Inquisitive," corrected Lottie.

"And you are?" Hetty asked the young man.

He stepped forwards and proffered his hand. "Harry Dale, son of your new licensees."

"Won't you be missed on the bar?" Kate asked.

"Not for a minute or two. I said I was going to the loo. Everyone is preoccupied at the moment anyway because the press have just arrived and they're taking pictures."

"The press are here! We better get back out there then," Lottie turned towards the door.

"When you say press, do you mean the real press or a chap from the Pentrillick Gazette?" Hetty asked.

"Both I think."

"Come on then let's go," Lottie opened the dining room door, "Meanwhile girls, I suggest you find this young man something to eat."

"Yeah, we will. Come with us, Harry. Benvolio will feed you." The girls each took one of his arms and led him towards the kitchen.

Back out in the bar, the ladies found Gideon standing with a tray in his hands looking lost. "There you are. Where have you been?" he grumbled, "I've been walking around with this tray looking and feeling a right lemon."

"Sorry, Gids," Debbie kissed his cheek, "we went exploring and sort of got held up."

"Well, while you were exploring several newspapermen arrived and they've taken loads of pictures including one of me with this tray."

Hetty looked all round. "Where are they now?"

"Outside with Clara. They're interviewing her about the bag she found today."

When they finished work in the kitchen, Benvolio and his waitresses went into the bar to join in with the celebrations. There was quite a party atmosphere and no-one wanted to leave

148

in case they missed something, especially gossip as regards the murder of Miranda Snow and the capture of the village's burglar. However, for Kate and Vicki there was another reason for them to stay at the pub: Harry Dale. For the twins, like the other two waitresses were smitten with the licensees' young son and all four vied for his attention as they sat as near to the bar as possible, fluttering their eyelashes, pouting their lips for selfies and sipping glasses of Coke.

"Oh to be young again," Debbie watched wistfully as the girls watched Harry, "although I'm sure when we were young we would have been a lot more subtle than youngsters are today."

"Yes, maybe," said Hetty, "but I think it's more like we hope we were more subtle but I doubt it. Remember we were teenagers in the Swinging Sixties and things have never been the same since."

"And tonight they're playing sixties music," said Debbie, "very apt."

Gideon glanced up at the two speakers on either end of the bar from which the music was playing. "I complimented James on his choice when I bought the drinks earlier and he said that because music from that era is known by young and old it seems the obvious choice to bring people together."

It was nearly one o'clock when James locked the front door of the pub after the last of the revellers had gone home.

"Well, that went better than I ever dared hope." He switched off the outside lights. "Anyone fancy a nightcap?"

Tess yawned. "Well, I shouldn't really because I'm due in the teashop at nine in the morning but it would be nice to sit down for a few minutes as my feet are killing me."

"Snap," groaned Ella, "but serves me right for wearing new shoes. And with heels too, not a good choice."

James laughed. "I told you not to, love. I mean, when you're behind the bar no-one can see your feet anyway. What's more, shoes get splashed with drinks."

"Yes, yes, I know," Ella lifted her right foot and looked at the sticky soles of her shoe, "Yuck. Anyway, I'll have a Baileys with ice, please, and you can wait on me." She sat down next to Tess and kicked off her shoes with disdain.

"How about you, Harry? Fancy a drink or are you ready for bed?" James reached to the top shelf for the bottle of Baileys.

"I'll have a drink, please, Dad. But I'm not ready for bed. To me the night is young."

"Yes, I suppose it is and it would have been with me when I was your age. Anyway, you did really well tonight considering you'd never worked on a bar before and as for you, Tess, I don't know how we would have managed without you. You're a star."

Ella agreed. "And Benvolio and the girls did well too. I heard several people raving about the buffet and the girls looked lovely even though I couldn't tell the Burton twins apart."

"I could," said Harry.

"How?"

"Admittedly, they look the same but when they open their mouths the difference is obvious. Kate speaks quietly, whereas Vicki is inclined to be loud."

"Oh, so you know their names already?" James chuckled.

"Of course, and the other two girls are Jade and Juliet."

Before they went to bed, Hetty and Lottie sat at their kitchen table drinking hot chocolate and eating bread pudding as both felt they needed to unwind.

"What a day," said Lottie, "my head still feels in a whirl."

"Mine too. I look forward to having a very lazy day tomorrow when perhaps we'll be able to piece together some of what we learned today."

"Yes, good idea because there is one thing puzzling me. It's about this Elliot Harris chap. I mean, if he was going around doing surveys why hadn't anyone recognised him?"

"That's a good point, Lottie. He called on Tommy and Kitty, didn't he? And they were nearly late for Sam and Martha's wedding. Which is odd because surely by now Kitty or Tommy would have seen him and made the connection."

"He also called on Debbie and Gideon. What's more he drove them to and from Marazion when they went out for their wedding anniversary meal. So why didn't they make the connection and recognise him as the survey man?"

"I don't know. It doesn't make sense." Hetty stood and placed her empty mug on the draining board.

"No, it doesn't, Het, and I think it might be best to forget about it for now as I'm sure we'll get an explanation before long."

Chapter Twenty-One

Elliot Harris, who denied he had had anything to do with any other robberies in Pentrillick prior to the one where he had been caught red-handed, lay on a bed in a police cell and considered his options. Should he come clean and confess or should he continue to protest his innocence? He turned onto his side and unrhythmically tapped the frame of the bed. If he were to confess then life would certainly be easier. No more lies or wild stories to conjure up. He might even get off with a lighter sentence. Whereas the prospect of denying all knowledge of his previous crimes would undoubtedly get him into hot water as he was bound to contradict himself at some point and make a bad situation even worse.

He propped himself up on his right arm, stared blankly at the bare floor and cursed the day a friend in Penzance had told him of his new part-time job doing surveys for a national firm. The job his friend claimed was a doddle; he enjoyed going out and about and meeting people and had recently been to the village where Elliot was currently living. Elliot's ears had pricked up when his friend described visiting a house in Blackberry Way with panoramic views over the village to the coast beyond. The couple who lived there were really friendly but he had had to cut his visit short as they were about to go to the wedding of their local vicar. When Elliot had shown interest, the friend had passed on details of the firm and suggested he apply for a part-time job to help with his finances. Elliot agreed. The extra money would be very useful and give him something to do in the daytime, for most people only required taxis in the evening.

It was when Elliot, who was prone to be light-fingered, made his first call that he saw the potential for returning to selected properties to purloin a few choice objects especially if he were able to establish through a little light-hearted chat a time when the householders might be out. However, he thought if he were to do so then he having visited the house would make him a potential suspect. To overcome this, he had made up the story of an attempted burglary at his rented home in Honeysuckle Drive, thus enabling him to give the police a description of the imaginary thief who looked nothing like himself.

After that it was easy and to make sure his identity was unknown to potential victims he made a point of not leaving details of either his or the survey firm's names at houses where he considered it likely that he might return for a nocturnal second visit. To eradicate all traces of his first visit he deleted the surveys completed by his chosen victims from his tablet so that the company for whom he worked knew nothing of his call.

Most of his calls were genuine and outside Pentrillick and he filled in their preferences diligently but occasionally, if he thought a house in the village looked a viable proposition and the owner occupier was unknown to him then he would risk a visit to suss the place out. This was what happened when he called at Sunnyside. The garden was overgrown and so he estimated the owner could well be elderly and quite possibly in the possession of a few valuables they wouldn't miss. He laid back his head on the pillow and tutted. "Big mistake, Elliot old boy. Big mistake."

As they stepped beneath the lichgate after church on Sunday morning, Hetty and Lottie glanced across the road to Sunnyside and waved to Betsy Triggs who was looking out of her sitting room window, delighted that the view was no longer obscured. Proud that they had been involved in the clearance of her garden, the sisters then strode off along the pavement towards the Old Bakehouse where they had been invited for Sunday lunch.

"Sandra's tubs and window boxes are looking stunning," said Lottie, as they approached the junction with Goose Lane.

"They certainly are. I do hope they win a prize." As they reached the tubs, Hetty brushed her hand over the tips of lavender to release the undistinguishable scent.

"Bill's hanging baskets are looking healthy too and the plants are smothered in flowers," observed Lottie, "I just hope the tomatoes that have set ripen in time."

Sandra greeted them as they stepped over the threshold. "Have you recovered from all the happenings on Friday?"

Lottie placed her handbag on the table while she unbuttoned her short sleeved jacket. "Just about. What a day that was."

"You can say that again. My throat still feels hoarse from all the chatter but it was wonderful to see everyone together under the same roof." Sandra closed the door.

"How are the twins getting on with the staff and new licensees?" Hetty asked.

"Very well. They're quite overwhelmed by Benvolio's talents and are absolutely besotted with young Harry."

Lottie chuckled. "Yes, we noticed that on Friday and he seems a nice lad."

"Zac told us something interesting last night. I nearly rang you but it was gone ten so I thought it a bit too late."

"Now that sounds intriguing," said Lottie.

"Anything to do with Miranda's unfortunate demise?" Hetty asked. "After all, that's the only mystery unsolved now."

"Yes, it is," Sandra brushed her hand over a ruck in the dining room tablecloth. "Anyway, we don't want to stand in here all morning but since we won't be eating for another hour or so because Bill's working and won't be back 'til one, would you like coffee and biscuits while I relay Zac's news?"

"Yes please."

"Let's go in the kitchen then because I have a loaf of bread in the oven and don't want to miss the timer pinging."

"Very apt for the Old Bakehouse," teased Hetty as she and Lottie followed Sandra into the kitchen and took seats on the stools at the breakfast bar.

Sandra switched on the kettle and took three mugs from a cupboard. "That's what Bill said when I told him I was making bread."

"So what's the news?" Hetty was eager to hear.

Sandra made the coffee and then sat down. "Well really it's just gossip but Zac told us that on the last night that the pub's tradesmen were here in the village, Sid was chatting to Vince in the hotel bar. You know who I mean, don't you? Vince was the chap who did the plastering and the woodwork too." The sisters both nodded. "Good. Anyway, Vince said that a few years ago when Gavin first joined the firm he jokingly told his new workmates that his wife to whom he had only just got married told him that if ever a chap with a Liverpudlian accent came looking for her to say emphatically that he didn't know her. Gavin reckoned he must have been an old boyfriend or something like that and he assumed they had fallen out. As far as Vince knows the Liverpudlian never turned up anyway and so nothing more was ever said."

"Hmm, I expect if she'd ditched the poor bloke he would have been bitter at first," reasoned Hetty, "but no doubt he soon got over it and met someone else. These things happen all the time. And remember, I knew three chaps many years ago

155

one of whom I thought might have been Mr Right but as you know nothing came of any of the romances."

"Their loss." Lottie had always felt that fate had been cruel to her sister who had never married.

Sandra laughed. "Yes, I agree. But as regards Miranda and the Liverpudlian, there must have been considerable animosity for her to have said what she did and when Gavin told Vince, Vince got the impression that Miranda was actually quite scared at the prospect of him turning up."

"So do you think this old boyfriend might be the one who took poor Miranda's life?" Lottie asked, "I mean, is that what you're suggesting?"

"I don't know but apparently Vince told the police about it the day after her death just in case it turned out to be murder. He thought it might help, you see. But that would have been well over a week ago now so I suppose it hasn't helped."

Hetty took a sip of coffee and then placed her mug on the breakfast bar. "Does Vince not know the name of this Liverpudlian chappie? I mean, surely Miranda would have mentioned it to Gavin when she first told him."

Sandra shook her head. "Sadly Vince didn't know although he admitted that Gavin might have mentioned it and he's just forgotten. After all it was a few years ago. Anyway, it might have nothing to do with the case but whatever, it's food for thought."

"It certainly is," agreed Lottie, "Having said that I can't recall the last time I heard a Liverpudlian accent, especially down here."

"That's just what I said to Bill. Last time I heard one would have been on the telly no doubt and probably a comedian."

"Or one of the two remaining Beatles," Hetty added.

"Talking of the telly, I hope you don't mind but we'll be making a dash after lunch because we want to get back to watch the Wimbledon Men's final this afternoon, don't we, Het?"

"We do. I never used to like tennis but now I'm retired and have time to watch it, I love it."

Sandra jumped up when the timer on the oven went off. "If you'd like to you can watch it here on our new smart TV. The reason why Bill is finishing at lunch time is so that he'll be back in time to see it. The children will be watching it and Emma's coming round too. So it'll be a nice big family affair. What's more I've made a chocolate fudge cake for the occasion."

When Hetty got ready for bed on Sunday evening her head was spinning with the day's activities: Vicar Sam's moving sermon, the floral displays throughout the village, Bill's hanging baskets, the latest gossip from Sandra and the excitement of the men's Wimbledon final which had lasted for a staggering four hours and fifty seven minutes. To help her sleep she opened her bedroom window; the curtains fluttered in the gentle breeze as she looked down onto the garden below where the petals of a white rose glowed in the light from her bedroom window.

Hoping that sleep would be imminent, she wearily climbed into bed but as she laid her head on the pillow she felt something niggling away at her brain. Was it something she had seen or something she had heard? Whatever it was she felt that it might be important. Unable to remember the cause of the niggling she finally drifted off to sleep after making a mental note to try and recall whatever it was first thing in the morning.

At six o'clock the following day, she suddenly awoke and remembered what it was. "A Liverpool accent," she muttered, "How can I have been so stupid?" With haste she leapt from her bed, grabbed her dressing gown from the hook on the door and dashed into Lottie's room.

"Wake up, Lottie."

Lottie was already awake. "What's up, Het?"

"Steve Frost has a Liverpudlian accent. I'd forgotten 'til now, but that's what Tess told me in the hotel bar. His name is Steve Frost, he's in insurance and has a Liverpool accent."

Lottie sat up. "What! You didn't tell us that."

Hetty looked embarrassed. "No and that's because I was too taken with the fact that he was in insurance and that his surname was the same as Miranda's maiden name. It just slipped my mind."

Lottie threw back her duvet and reached for her slippers. "Let's go downstairs. I could do with a cup of tea."

When tea was made they both sat down at the table in the kitchen.

"Right, I've had time to think about it," said Lottie, "and I should imagine that when Vince told the police about threats to Miranda from a Liverpudlian, they would have looked into it. Do you agree with that?"

"Yes, I suppose so and that's what Sandra said she assumed had happened, didn't she? But then it's likely that the police knew nothing of Steve Frost. In fact, they've probably never even heard of him. And why should they? According to Sandra, Vince couldn't remember or wasn't sure if he'd even been told the name of the mysterious Liverpudlian so they wouldn't have been looking for a Steve Frost, would they?"

"No," answered Lottie, "of course not, but they would have tried to find out something about the mysterious Liverpudlian by questioning Miranda's friend and partner in crime. You know, Patty or whatever she's called. I mean, surely if she's cooperating with the police and wants to help find Miranda's killer then she would have been only too happy to tell of any boyfriends Miranda had had."

Hetty leaned her head back against the wall. "Yes, of course. You're right, Lottie. What a relief."

"It still doesn't mean that Steve Frost's not involved though, does it? I mean, we know he's in insurance and shares Miranda's maiden name so there could have been a fiddle there somewhere. Assuming they're related, that is."

"Yes, but then taking your stance, I daresay the police will have looked into that too. You know, checked out her close relatives and so forth."

"Precisely, and if a close relative worked for the same insurance company that Gavin was insured with they'd soon have smelt a rat."

"Thank goodness, so I think it's time we admitted, Lottie, that Steve Frost is nothing more than an associate of Clara Bragg despite his accent."

"Yes, on the other hand, he still might have killed her but for reasons unknown. Unknown to us anyway. In fact the police might have him under arrest as we speak because if you think about it, he's about the right size to fit into the clothes that Clara found in Betsy's garden."

"Yes, but if he is involved where does Clara Bragg fit into all this? And was Steve even here when Miranda was killed?" Hetty stood and put the kettle on for another cup of tea.

"He was definitely here when Miranda was killed but I'm not sure about Clara's role in this. Perhaps they're making sure they're seen together so they can provide each other with alibis, should it be necessary."

"Could be. It does seem odd that Clara found the bag in Betsy's garden though. I mean, let's be honest, if she was involved then surely they would never have hidden the clothes there knowing that the Gardening Club were going to tidy it up."

"That's a very good point, Het, but I think for now it's best if we say nothing and just keep an eye on Clara and Steve."

"I agree, but we'll share our thought with Debbie and Kitty and see if they have any bright ideas."

On Monday evening, the Gardening Club met for their weekly gathering and as Sandra and Bill were about to take their seats, Sandra caught sight of Clara heading in their direction. As she went to take a seat beside Bill, Sandra swung him round so that he sat on the end of the row. Sandra then sat down beside Clara.

"Oh, hello, Clara, I didn't see you there," Sandra smiled sweetly.

"Really?" Clara was clearly not amused.

Sandra crossed her legs. "I'm glad I've seen you because I really must congratulate you on your tubs, hanging baskets and so forth. You see, I walked along Church Row and past your house the other day, Clara, and I was most impressed with your gazanias." She laughed, "They're stunning and I must admit doing a lot better than the ones in the care home garden but then I suppose slugs might have had a feast on them."

Clara went very pale and was saved from responding by Sally who clapped her hands and then welcomed everyone to the meeting after which she said that she had two announcements to make.

"Firstly, I have received a lovely letter from Betsy Triggs thanking you all for the wonderful work you did and saying how much she enjoyed your company. So for that I think you should feel very proud."

"I know Lottie and I didn't do any physical work but it was a privilege to be there," gushed Hetty, "and I think I speak for everyone when I say that we really enjoyed every minute of it. Talk about never a dull moment."

Those who had been at Sunnyside echoed Hetty's words.

Sally nodded. "Good, now secondly, I've been informed by the police that they have been able to obtain DNA from the balaclava we, or rather you, Clara, found in the garden at Sunnyside and therefore there is to be a voluntary DNA testing to check all males in the village to see if they can find a match."

Several people gasped.

"But surely the guilty person is unlikely to volunteer," reasoned Veronica.

Sally removed her reading glasses. "I agree and I suppose if that were the case then he would have a guilty finger pointed at him. In fact that's probably what the police are hoping will happen. I daresay they'll have a list of all males in the village and tick them off as they come forwards."

"That's assuming he lives in the village," said Tess, "I mean surely there's nothing at all to indicate that. Miranda wasn't from around here, was she? So why should her killer be?"

Sally nodded. "I agree, so perhaps if they have no luck in the village they'll take their search further afield."

"It's probably a silly question but how do they know the DNA is that of a male?" Bill asked.

Sally shrugged her shoulders. "It's not a silly question but I really don't know the answer, Bill. I'm not very scientific and so when it comes to that sort of stuff I'm way out of my depth."

"Perhaps the DNA would reveal it," Clara suggested.

"Maybe," said Kitty, "or perhaps they're simply going by the fact that the black jacket you found, Clara, was a man's size large."

"Is there any news about the taxi chap who was caught at Betsy's place on Thursday night?" Maisie asked, "Several people have mentioned it in the shop but no-one seems to know the latest."

Sally shook her head. "I've no idea. Does anyone know anything?"

"I know he's home because I saw him in his garden yesterday but not to speak to," said Veronica.

"That's right, he is," Tess agreed, "What's more he has confessed and handed over all stolen goods to the police including the money from the farm robbery none of which he had spent. He has also agreed to pay for the windows that he broke to be repaired. Without doubt he's full of remorse and wishes that he could turn back the clock."

"How do you know this?" Veronica asked.

"Because yesterday I went to see Betsy to ask her when she'd like us to tackle her back garden and we got talking about Elliot Harris. She told me that now the drama's all over and done with she can't stop thinking about him and how nice he was. She also said that she doubted anyone would use his taxi service again, especially after he's sentenced and she wondered what might become of him. I was so touched by her concern that on my way home I made a note of his number as I passed the post office window. I then rang him and booked a taxi to Penzance. I didn't need to go there and I would normally drive anyway but I wanted to speak to him to hear what he had to say. When I got home I rang Betsy and told her what I'd done. She was really sweet and said that everyone deserves a second chance."

Chapter Twenty-Two

Late on Tuesday afternoon, as Ashley Rowe, erstwhile landlord of the Crown and Anchor, sat staring at his laptop, he heard a car pull up outside and so assumed that his wife Alison was home from a day at the school where she taught. The car doors slammed and then he heard her key in the Yale lock. He stood to greet her as she entered the kitchen with bulging bags of shopping in both hands.

"Here, let me help you," Ashley sprang forwards, took the bags from her hands and placed them on the kitchen work surface.

"Thank you," Alison removed her lightweight cardigan and hung it on a peg by the back door. "I see you were working. How's the book coming on?"

Ashley sat back down in his swivel chair. "Fine, fine, thanks, although I appear to have writer's block today."

"Oh dear. Anyway, sorry I'm late but I knew several things were running low so thought I might as well go into the supermarket since I pass it on my way home." She took a chilli plant from one of the bags and placed it on the kitchen window sill in the sun. "Why are you scowling, Ash?"

"Am I? Sorry I didn't realise I was."

Alison took her handbag from the table and placed it on top of a bookcase, she then sat down at the kitchen table opposite her husband. "Yes, I noticed that you were scowling when I came in and you still are. Something's bothering you. Come on, tell me what it is."

"It's nothing."

"For heaven's sake, Ash, we've been married for years and I know when something's not right."

"Yes, I suppose you do."

"So what is it? Is it the book?"

"No, no, it's not the book, it's just that a while ago I was thinking back over events that happened during the time we had the pub and then this latest incident sprang to mind. You know, the murder of that poor woman in the hotel bath. So I Googled it and read all about it, then something in the back of my mind told me that I know something that will help solve it but for the life of me I can't think what it can be."

"Really, but that makes no sense. I mean, apart from going to Vicar Sam's wedding we've not been back to Pentrillick, have we?"

"I know, you're right, but…."

"I think that whatever it is you must have dreamt it. I mean, your imagination must be working overtime at the moment with the book and so forth."

"Yes, you're probably right."

"I'm sure I am. After all your book is influenced by the years we were in the pub and so it's obvious that Pentrillick will be on your mind even when you're sleeping."

"Yes, but…" Ashley sat up straight. "No, no, listen, we have been there recently. Remember we saw Tess in the supermarket a while back and she told us how attractive the village was looking because of the Pentrillick in Bloom competition and so we drove through on our way back from Helston one day to see the flowers."

"Ah, yes, of course, you're right. We did, but what of it?"

Ashley stood up and crossed to the window. "It's coming back, Alison. Something happened along the main street."

"Did it? It can't have been very momentous then because I don't remember seeing anything other than flowers, houses and shops. And of course, our old pub. We mustn't forget that, must we?"

Ashley sat back down and closed his eyes. "No, but whatever it was, was before the pub."

"Oh, well, sorry, I can't really help." Alison stood and began to put away the groceries. As she opened a cupboard door, Ashley suddenly leapt to his feet. "Yes of course, that's it. I've remembered now. It's the rope, Alison, it's the rope."

"Rope?"

"Yes, in the report it said that the police reckoned the murderer used a rope to climb into the hotel window and that it was probably stolen from the village charity shop. Well, that's where the memory is. I've a vague recollection of someone standing outside the shop holding a rope of some sort as we drove by. Don't you remember? It's less than two weeks ago."

Alison shook he head. "No, definitely not. I would have been looking at the flowers. I mean, some of the displays were quite stunning."

Ashley growled and paced the room. "Yes, they were. Oh how frustrating. If only I could remember."

Alison opened the door of the refrigerator. "Well I'm sorry but I can't help. Sadly I don't have a photographic memory."

"Photographic. That's it. The dash cam. Well done." Ashley gave her a hug and then rushed out of the house; minutes later he returned with the camera in his hands. "If I'm right, Alison, the image will have been captured on here."

His hands shook as he connected the camera to his laptop, they both then sat and watched the footage. It didn't take long as Ashley seldom went out and so the day in question came up quickly. To Alison's surprise her husband was right. Standing outside the charity shop was a man tucking a coil of rope into a large carrier bag and furtively looking over his shoulder as he did so.

Ashley froze the image.

"Have you any idea who he is?" Alison asked.

"Not the foggiest so we'll have to leave it to the police to find out."

"Are you going to ring them?"

Ashley leaned back in his chair. "I'm not sure. I could do that or it might be easier if I drove over to Camborne and dropped the camera off at the police station myself."

"That's a good idea. I'll go with you if you do and then on the way back we can grab a takeaway unless you feel like knocking something up. I've had a busy day and don't feel like cooking, especially now after what you've just discovered."

"Me neither, far too much on my mind and so we'll do as you say. Meanwhile I'll make us both a cup of tea. It might help stop my hands from shaking."

Inside the police station, Detective Inspector Fox sat at his desk and read through reports and details of the Miranda Snow murder case. Her death puzzled him. She had been their prime suspect as regards the murder of her husband, Gavin; after all, she had a motive and were it not for her rock solid alibi, she would have been arrested soon after the crime had taken place, but he could see no motive for anyone to have taken her life. Admittedly, there was allegedly someone with a Liverpudlian accent who might have borne a grudge, but without a name it was impossible to trace the man in question, and as for her friends, it seemed none of them knew anything of him: if he existed they never met or saw him. Even her closest friend, Patty Thompson, was unaware of a boyfriend from Liverpool, although she admitted that she knew nothing of Miranda's associates up-country for the short time she was away from Cornwall. Was he then a figment of her imagination? When she told her husband of him was it to appear a damsel in distress? It was unlikely they would ever find out and even if

166

they did and the man in question existed, the fact that he bore a grudge against her was hardly a motive for murder. And then there was the rope which appears to have been taken from the charity shop. Was that the rope used? If so who took it? They weren't even sure that a rope was the means of entering the victim's room. It could have been a ladder but all thought it was highly unlikely. A person walking through the village with a ladder on his shoulder could hardly be missed. And the window was definitely where he had made his entrance because there were fresh breaks in the honeysuckle stems and part of the wooden trellis was broken. Besides, CCTV showed that no-one entered Miranda Snow's room through the door on the night she died so the window was the only possible place of entry. As he closed the file there was a knock on his door.

"Come in," he growled.

Police sergeant Amy Thomas entered the room and he saw that she was smiling.

"Sir, we have Mr and Mrs Ashley Rowe downstairs who have something of great interest regarding the Snow case. Shall I send them up?"

A smile crossed the face of Detective Inspector Fox. "Yes, Amy. Please do."

On Tuesday evening, Hetty, Lottie and Debbie went to the Crown and Anchor after bingo.

"Oh, what a treat to be back in the old routine." Lottie kicked off her shoes as they sat down at a table by the fire where a huge display of dried grasses filled the hearth.

"And there are some very tempting smells wafting out from the dining room," commented Hetty, "Makes me feel hungry even though I'm not."

Lottie looked at the 'specials' menu on a chalk board beside the French doors. "Perhaps another week instead of eating before we go out we could eat here after bingo. I'd certainly like to sample the new chef's food because the nibbles he put out on the opening night were absolutely delicious."

"Good idea," agreed Debbie, "I wonder what time they serve food 'til."

Hetty pointed to a notice above the bar. "Ten o'clock Sunday to Friday and eleven on Saturday."

"Ideal," Debbie gleefully rubbed her hands together, "we could easily make it then because we're usually out of bingo by a quarter past nine."

"Good, that's something to look forward to then." Lottie hoped the prawn, garlic and chilli linguine on the specials board would still be available the following week.

Later, when Debbie went to the bar for more drinks she realised that she was standing next to Steve Frost the insurance man with whom Clara had been seen at the hotel and who spoke with a Liverpudlian accent. Recalling Hetty and Lottie considered the possibility of him being an old boyfriend and therefore a suspect as regards the death of Miranda Snow, she decided to probe a little; her confidence boosted by the two glasses of wine she had already consumed. "Hello, I've seen you before at the hotel with Clara. Are you on holiday?"

"Yes, I've been here for a month now looking into more business outlets so it's been a sort of working holiday. Sadly it's now time to go home though, more's the shame."

Debbie rested one elbow on the bar. "Oh, poor you. Anyway, at least you've had some lovely weather while you've been here."

"Yes, I've been very lucky. I'm a bit of a sun worshipper so being here has enabled me to top up my tan. Much better than using sun beds."

"So will you have gone home before tomorrow?" It occurred to Debbie that if he was leaving he would avoid the DNA testing the police were to do in the village.

He looked at his watch. "Before tomorrow? That might be difficult as it's a quarter past ten now and so nearly tomorrow already, but for what it's worth I go home on Thursday." Steve, puzzled by her strange question, slowly took a bank debit card from his wallet.

From the corner of her eye, Debbie saw that Tess was pouring two drinks. She glanced around the bar. "Is Clara not with you tonight?"

"Yes, she's gone to powder her nose, as my mum used to say. Is she a friend of yours?" Steve decided Debbie was harmless and it was the wine talking.

"Yes, no, well yes, sort of. Most people in the village are friends, you see. She's not been here long though but I know her through the Gardening Club which has only just started."

Steve groaned. "So I've heard. Clara is rather an enthusiast when it comes to gardening and that's putting it mildly. It seems to be her favourite subject. In fact sometimes it's her only subject."

"Have you known her long?"

"All my life. Well, not quite all. We used to go to school together many moons ago but lost touch after we left. I couldn't believe it when I bumped into her the other day. I didn't even know she was living in Cornwall."

"Oh, oh, I see. So your reunion wasn't planned then?"

"Oh, by all means no. Can I buy you and your friends a drink?" Steve quickly glanced towards the table where Hetty and Lottie, caught off guard when they saw him look in their direction, both inspected their fingernails and tried to act normally. Amused by their discomfort he smothered a smile.

"No, no, that's very kind, but thank you for the offer." Debbie wanted to ask about insurance but couldn't think of a subtle way to bring the subject up and time ran out when Tess placed Steve's drinks on the bar. He waved his card over the paying device, thanked Tess and nodded to Debbie.

"Refills?" Tess asked as Steve walked out through the open French doors and onto the sun terrace; simultaneously, Clara emerged from the Ladies.

"Yes, yes, please, Tess." Debbie nodded towards the French doors, "We reckon that that Steve chap you just served is something to do with the insurance firm that Gavin Snow had his life insurance with and that he and Miranda are, were, related."

"Yes, Hetty said something along those lines the other day when I was working at the hotel."

"Exactly and so do you reckon like us that he pulled a few strings to make sure she got the pay out?"

"Well no, because she didn't, did she?" Tess smiled mischievously.

"What?"

"Miranda didn't get the pay out, did she?"

"Oh, no, that's true, but even if she didn't live long enough to get the money they still might have been in it together. Although we have to admit the police must have looked into it."

Tess leaned over the bar. "I don't think you're on the right track, Debbie. Earlier this evening before you got here, he and Clara were sitting at the bar and he was telling her how he's thinking of changing his job because he doesn't really like selling car insurance."

It was just after eleven when the ladies finished their last drinks; they were reluctant to leave for they had enjoyed seeing faces old and new coming and going throughout the evening. As they stood to gather their things together, Ella walked around the bar collecting empty glasses. "Are you, ladies off now?" she asked.

"Regrettably, yes," said Hetty, "we think we've had enough wine for one evening. In fact we've had more than we usually do on a Tuesday night."

Smiling sweetly, Ella picked up their empty glasses. "Good for us then but probably not so good for you."

Debbie chuckled. "It'll have been worth it because we had to celebrate being back in the old routine."

"I've seen you before, haven't I? You were in on our opening night. So do you live in the village?"

Lottie nodded. "Yes, and you probably don't know, but your waitresses Vicki and Kate are my granddaughters."

"Really! So you must be Sandra's mum."

"Bill's actually."

"I see, so you'll be a Mrs Burton."

"That's right. Charlotte Burton, known as Lottie, and this is my twin sister, Henrietta known as Hetty." Lottie rested her hand on Debbie's shoulder, "and this dear lady is our very good friend, Debbie Elms."

"Well I'm delighted to meet you all and hope we'll see you again soon."

"No question about that," laughed Hetty, "Tuesdays haven't been the same these last few months and we're thrilled to bits now that you're open again."

They all wished Ella goodnight and then left the pub by the front door.

"Hmm, the evening smells gorgeous," gushed Debbie as they stepped out onto the pavement, "The combination of the jasmine, the night scented stock and the sea is pure delight."

"Let's take a wander through the pub's garden before we go home," suggested Lottie, "we can see perfectly well as there's a full moon and I'm not in the least bit tired."

They wandered into the gardens and sat down at one of the picnic tables by a border of golden flowers.

171

"It seems that every garden has a show of rudbeckias this year," observed Debbie, "It must be a good summer for them."

"Yes, ours are doing really well although they did get a bit battered by the recent wind," admitted Lottie, "so we might have to prop them up before the competition gets judged."

"I'm hearing what you're both saying," said Hetty, "but look over there, there's a light on in that caravan and it can't be any of the tradesmen because they've all long gone home."

Lottie looked in the direction her sister's hand pointed. "It'll be the new chef, Benvolio Moretti or whatever he's called. Remember, Sandra told us that the twins said he's living on site. When he first got here he was in one of the pub's old guest rooms but I suppose he prefers to be out here so he's a bit more independent."

Hetty nodded. "Yes, of course. Silly me."

"And I suppose James and Ella will want the rooms anyway for paying guests with the holiday season just around the corner," reasoned Debbie.

"According to the twins, he might buy one of the new houses in due course and get his mum down here to live," Lottie added.

"That's nice, meanwhile he has this for a temporary home. I don't know about you ladies but I could quite happily live out here in a caravan during the summer months." Debbie looked to the clear night sky where countless stars twinkled around the full moon.

Hetty nodded. "Me too."

"What's that over there?" Lottie pointed beyond a rose bed, "I saw movement under that table."

"Probably some small creature having a feast on food dropped by humans," muttered Debbie.

Lottie stood up. "I'm going to see. It might be a badger."

Hetty laughed. "More like a cat or a dog."

Nevertheless, Debbie and Hetty followed Lottie in the direction she had indicated. As they reached the table, a fox turned to face them; he then ran off over the fields.

"Wow, I've never seen a real fox before," Debbie hurriedly climbed up onto the table and watched until he was out of sight.

The sudden sound of a male voice caused them to turn their heads. The silhouette of a man was standing beside an open window in the caravan. "Hi Mum," they heard a voice say, "Sorry it's late but I've not long been finished work." There was a pause, then, "Yeah, yeah, everything here is fine. Love the work, love the pub and love the people. I'm going to miss watching the Reds' matches next season though but then I can't have everything and I can always watch their games on the telly instead."

"That'll be the new chef on the phone to his mum," whispered Lottie, "that's really sweet."

Hetty shook her head. "It's not, Lottie. Benvolio Moretti is supposed to be Italian, whoever that is in there has a Liverpudlian accent."

Lottie's jaw dropped. "A Liverpudlian accent, but…"

"Exactly."

As Hetty's voice faded, the phone call ended and they heard footsteps crossing the caravan floor.

"Quick hide," squeaked Lottie.

The sisters helped Debbie down from the table they then all dashed towards the car park and hid behind a car where they watched as the caravan door opened. From it stepped the chef singing, 'You'll Never Walk Alone'.

Chapter Twenty-Three

The three ladies continued to crouch behind the car too afraid to move. The chef, meanwhile remained on the steps of his caravan and took a packet of cigarettes from the pocket of his trousers.

"Oh no," Hetty whispered, "don't say he's going to stay there while he smokes. My legs feel like they're about to give way."

"Kneel down," hissed Lottie, "that's what I'm doing, the tarmac's not too hard."

From behind, the pub door opened and four people unknown to the ladies stepped out onto the pavement. Debbie gasped. "Oh, no, please tell me this isn't their car."

To her relief the strangers stayed outside the pub and chatted loudly beneath the Crown and Anchor sign; after a few minutes, a taxi pulled up alongside the pavement and took them away.

"Phew," Lottie heaved a great sigh of relief, "that was close."

Benvolio finished his cigarette, threw the butt onto the grass, stretched his arms and then walked slowly around the gardens. When he reached the picnic table where the ladies had recently sat, he took a seat.

"I don't think he'll be able to see us now because he's looking the other way so let's make a dash for it," Hetty scrambled to her feet.

"But where to?" Lottie asked, "We need to phone the police."

"Anywhere but here."

"Let's creep over to the pub door," urged Debbie, "We can then talk in loud stage whispers and pretend we've just come out. That way if he looks over here and sees us he'll think nothing of it."

The sisters agreed and they all crept over towards the front entrance of the pub.

"I love the pub now," laughed Debbie, as she pretended to button up her jacket, "although I think I've probably had one too many."

"Me too," Lottie's laugh was self-conscious and sounded like a poor rendition of machine gun fire.

"We really must have a meal here another day because I'm told the food is fantastic," shouted Hetty, "James is so lucky to have found a *real* Italian chef."

"Don't push your luck, Het," Lottie hissed through gritted teeth, "He might think you're taking the micky. Remember he could well be dangerous."

The chef still sat at the picnic table as with arms linked, the ladies crossed the road and walked part-way up Long Lane. When they were out of earshot, Hetty took her phone from her handbag in order to ring the police.

"What was that?" Debbie asked, before Hetty had punched in 999, "Did you hear tyres screeching?"

Lottie looked down the lane towards the village but a bend in the road blocked her view. "I did and I think we better go and check. Benvolio might be doing a runner."

Hetty dropped her phone into her pocket and ran with her sister and friend back down the hill. To their relief, lights were still on in the chef's caravan and they could hear him moving around but a car was now parked by its side. The three ladies crept along the road and back into the pub gardens; as they hid amongst amusements in the children's play area they watched as a man stepped from the car and stood at the bottom of the caravan steps.

"Come out, Benvolio Moretti. I just saw you so I know you're in there."

Lottie gasped. "Oh my god, he's got a gun."

The man held the gun behind his back as the caravan door slowly opened and Benvolio stood on the top step. "Who the devil are you?"

"Felix."

"Felix. Felix who?" Benvolio folded his arms as if to emphasise his lack of interest.

"I don't think it really matters."

Benvolio laughed. "Okay, so what do you want, Felix I-don't-think-it really-matters?"

"Revenge." He moved his hand from behind his back and pointed the gun at the chef.

Benvolio took a step backwards.

"No," screamed Hetty, "too many people have already died." Without thinking, she leapt from her place of hiding, grabbed the small anchor from the flower bed, ran towards the caravan and before he had a chance to turn around, she hit the gunman over the head. He shrieked in pain and then fell to the ground, out flat.

Benvolio laughed. "Thank you, Granny. You've saved me the effort. Time now to make a hasty exit I think before Felix here comes round." He dashed into the caravan and slammed the door shut.

Hetty stood trembling. The gunman was motionless and she feared he was dead.

Debbie ran towards Hetty. "Throw me your phone, Het, and I'll ring the police."

Hetty, a quivering wreck, did as she was asked. Debbie rang 999.

The ladies remained in situ as Benvolio crashed and banged around inside the caravan. A few minutes later he rushed out pushing a few of his belongings into a rucksack.

"Hold it there," Lottie had the gun in her hands.

"You wouldn't shoot me," he laughed.

"Don't push your luck, sonny." After three large glasses of wine, Lottie was on autopilot.

The chef ignored her and walked towards the car park where his BMW stood beside a low wall. He stopped dead when he heard a bang and sensed something hit the ground by his feet.

"Drop the bag," commanded Lottie, "and raise your hands."

To her relief, he did as she asked. Simultaneously two police cars pulled into the car park. As four officers stepped from the cars, Lottie fainted.

Hetty knelt down beside her sister as Debbie explained briefly what they had heard and seen. One police officer thanked them as another put handcuffs on Benvolio Moretti. Within minutes two ambulances and more police were on the scene and the area was a sea of flashing blue lights.

As the chef was escorted to one of the cars, the last people remaining in the pub came out to see what the noise was about. When James and Ella saw their chef in handcuffs, James' jaw dropped in disbelief. "What the hell's going on?" Ella felt faint and sat on the side of the tub containing night scented stock.

Two officers approached the licensees and said they needed to ask them a few questions. James nodded, took his wife's hand and they all went inside the pub.

Lottie meanwhile having come round, sat in the back of the ambulance where Ivor, the paramedic held her shaking hands. On the ground outside the caravan more paramedics knelt beside Felix the gunman.

"Is he alive?" Hetty asked, as tears streamed down her face, "Please tell me he's not dead."

"Yes, it's not as bad as it looks and I don't think it'll be long before he comes round."

"Thank goodness. I'm such a fool I could have killed him."

Debbie having never seen Hetty cry, gave her friend a tight hug.

"And I could have killed the chef," sobbed Lottie, "I can't believe I fired that beastly gun at him."

The police officer holding the gun held it up in the light shining from inside the ambulance. He smiled. "I don't think this would have killed anyone, sweetheart. It's a replica toy gun."

To prove the point he unloaded small yellow balls into his hand.

Chapter Twenty-Four

Benvolio Moretti nervously sat in an interview room at the police station waiting to be questioned by Detective Inspector Fox and as he waited he contemplated what he would or should say. Should he confess to the murder of Miranda Snow or should he deny it? If he confessed he might receive a lighter prison sentence after all he was guilty and no doubt if it came to a trial the jury would find him so.

He looked at the two empty chairs on the opposite side of the desk and groaned. Could he really face hours of questioning? Hours of lying? He sighed deeply. If only he had not seen Miranda that night as he sat in the hotel bar with James and Ella. She didn't see him of course as she came staggering into the vestibule clearly drunk. But he saw her through the open door of the bar and had watched as she had teetered off down a passage towards the guest rooms. Had their eyes met then she might still be alive and in police custody instead of him. What a fool he was. All that needed to be done was for him to have informed the police of her crime and to say that after weeks, months and years of searching he had finally found her and that he wanted to press charges.

Of course, it would not help his case that he had never reported her crime: the reason, because he was too embarrassed. In fact he had told no-one, not even his widowed mother, that Miranda was a thief who had left him while he was working one evening and cleared his bank account of the money he had recently inherited from his grandparents. Money he intended to invest in a property as they had hoped. How she did it he would never know but since his arrival in Pentrillick he had heard it said on the grapevine that she had worked for a bank and so he assumed that knowledge had aided her thievery. Although if he were honest he had to admit there was little the police could have acted on, for the only evidence he had of her crime was a note that she had left on top of his laptop which read: *I've gone and you'll never find me. Thanks for the money, I'll spend it wisely. Lol. Miranda.*

Benvolio's mind drifted back over the years. He had known her for only a few weeks when she disappeared and before that he had enjoyed her company. She made him laugh and so when she told him that her landlord wanted to sell the flat where she lived, he believed her and to offer her a home seemed the obvious thing to do. She readily accepted and moved in with him two days later. Her possessions were little more than a few bags of clothes and toiletries. She told him that most of her belongings were still at the home of her parents but she never said where that home was and he never thought to ask.

So when she was gone, the lack of knowledge made his quest more difficult. Knowing nothing of her past, her friends or even her work colleagues he began a search and was disappointed further when he enquired at the building society where she claimed to have worked only to be told that no-one of that name did or ever had worked there. And so began a search that went on for years: a search that seemed fruitless. It appeared that she had vanished into thin air. Then unbeknown to him she must have come to Cornwall, married Gavin Snow and changed her name making his search for her even more difficult.

Benvolio thought of Gavin. Had she really killed him just to get the insurance money as village gossip said that her friend Patty claimed? He thought it more than possible, in which case he had got off lightly and in a way maybe he had won in the end, for in drowning her he had avenged not just the theft of the money from his bank account but the taking of poor Gavin's life too. Not that drowning her had been his original intention. His plan had been to strangle her while she was sleeping. To establish which room was hers he had watched the hotel from time to time hoping to see her at one of the windows. His surveillance paid off as the night before he took her life, he witnessed her arrive back at the hotel in a taxi, drunk again. Shortly after he saw the light come on in a room on the second floor and he caught sight of her walking past the window. On seeing the trellis that ran up the wall he noted the pegs to which it was attached - a much more secure holding for the rope than the sill he had originally planned to use.

Having already acquired a length of rope to scale the wall, he decided to return the following night and when he saw the candlelight flickering through the blind and realised she would be taking a bath, he decided to act promptly rather than wait until she retired to bed.

Warmed by the sun that shone in through a small sash window in the police interview room, he rolled up the sleeves of his cotton shirt. On his left arm he caught sight of the tattoo bearing his widowed mother's name, Sophia. Tears welled in his eyes as he thought of the shame he was about to bring to her and his family. Should he lie to protect them? To give them hope? But he knew it was a question he had no need to ponder over for his mother had always said that honesty was the best policy. His mother whose dreams of a new life in Cornwall were about to be dashed and replaced with news that her son, her only beloved son, was a cold blooded murderer.

A knock on the door caused the police officer watching over him to let someone in. Benvolio stood as the man he assumed to be his solicitor entered the room. On introduction, both men shook hands and then sat down side by side. Benvolio cleared his throat. "Before you say anything, sir, I must tell you that I have decided to confess. I murdered Miranda Snow. It was premeditated and carefully thought out but at the time I considered I had good reason."

Hetty, Lottie and Debbie spent several hours at the police station on Wednesday morning giving statements and in the evening, Bill, Sandra, Zac and the twins looked on in disbelief as they were shown footage on Hetty's phone of the events on Tuesday night.

"Debbie's brain must have been thinking really quick for her to have thought to record this," said Sandra, "I'm sure I'd have been far too scared to do anything as useful."

"Me too," Hetty agreed, "I was useless but Debbie said that having rung the police the phone was already in her hand and so it seemed the obvious thing to do."

"I was useless too," admitted Lottie, "I fainted. What a wuss."

Sandra patted her mother-in-law's hand. "I think I might have done the same."

"Just as well there was a full moon last night," said Vicki, matter of factually, "otherwise we'd not be able to see much at all."

"Have you shown it to the police?" Kate asked.

"Oh, yes and they were very pleased with the footage and have taken a copy," said Lottie, "as it gives an accurate account of exactly what occurred before they arrived. Although of course, Hetty hitting the gunman over the head with the anchor happened before Debbie rang the police."

"Thank goodness for that," groaned Hetty, "I wouldn't like a reminder of that on my phone. I really thought I'd killed him."

Lottie, having seen the video several times, leaned back in the sofa where she sat. "The police were ever so pleased the way things worked out because apparently last night someone handed them footage of a man tucking a coil of rope into a carrier bag outside the charity shop. It appears the footage was taken on a dash cam and they were in the process of printing off pictures taken from it. Then this morning they were going to start house to house enquiries to see if anyone recognised him so we've saved them the time and effort."

Bill, who sat between his mother and his aunt put his arms around their shoulders. "I'm very proud of you both, what stars you are. As for you, Mum. Never in a million years would I have thought I'd ever see you holding a gun let alone firing it. Mind you, I'm glad it wasn't real as you might have killed the poor man."

Lottie half-smiled. "I don't know what came over me but I was so cross and felt I couldn't let him get away, especially realising he might have killed Miranda. On reflection though I suppose three large glasses of wine might have given me Dutch courage. As for me killing him, had the gun been real, I think that prospect highly unlikely as my aim is pretty poor. I can't even hit the dart board in the right place and that's when I'm stone-cold sober."

"Could have been a case of beginner's luck though," teased Zac, "We often see that at the pub. Along comes someone who has never played pool before, we give them a game and they win easily. We sign them up for the team and then find that they're absolutely useless."

"You and your pool matches," laughed Sandra.

"Anyway," said Bill, "it appears the chef did kill poor Miranda and so all three of you should be very proud of your actions, even if they were out of character."

"I hardly think Miranda should be referred to as poor," scoffed Kate, "After all the dreadful woman was a murderer."

"And a fraud," Hetty added, "we mustn't forget that it was the insurance pay-out she was after."

"True," acknowledged Bill, "very true."

"I wonder what will happen to Felix, whoever he is, and the chef of course," pondered Hetty, "We know Benvolio is a murderer and so will face trial for that but as far as I can see, Felix did nothing more than threaten the chef with a replica toy gun. What's more, we don't even know why he threatened him."

"Or for that matter why Benvolio killed Miranda," Lottie added.

Sandra looked at the clock and realising it was nearly time for work, stood up. "I suppose we'll hear in due course as nothing stays quiet for long in this village."

In the early hours of Wednesday morning, Felix Ash came round to find that he was in a hospital bed under police watch. When doctors deemed he was well enough to answer questions, Detective Inspector Fox took a seat beside his bed; while in the corridor outside the room, a police constable stood by the door.

Because he had threatened Benvolio Moretti with a replica toy gun he could not be charged with possession of an offensive weapon. However the inspector was eager to learn the reason for his threats as he hoped by doing so it might fill in a few of the missing pieces in the jigsaw concerning the Snow murders.

Later that day he was discharged from hospital but rather than go home and face questions from his friends and family, he decided to stay in Pentrillick for a few days to think over what had happened and so he booked one of the new rooms at the Crown and Anchor.

On Thursday morning, Kitty knocked on the door of Primrose Cottage, Lottie answered and led her into the sitting room.

"Good, you're here as well, Debbie so I can tell all of you the latest news at the same time." She looked smug as she took a seat at the table.

"News," repeated Hetty, "what about the recent goings-on?"

Kitty nodded. "Yes, I have the very latest. Hot off the press as they say."

"Wait a tick while I make tea." Lottie ran from the room to put the kettle on. Hetty followed to speed up the process. When tea was made and they were all seated around the sitting room table, Kitty began her yarn.

"Well, I'm sure you'll be pleased to hear that Felix is on the mend and out of hospital and after a brief interview with the police he was not charged with any offence. He did admit that he had threatened Benvolio with a replica gun but that was just to scare him, the reason being he firmly believed that Benvolio had taken Miranda Snow's life."

"Which of course we now know he had," added Debbie.

Kitty nodded. "Precisely."

"I take it he must have known Miranda then," Lottie reasoned.

"Oh, yes, he did and what's more he has confessed to having had an affair with her."

"Really," tutted Lottie, "that girl goes down even lower in my estimation then."

"I agree," said Debbie, "Is there nothing she wouldn't stoop to?"

Kitty shrugged her shoulders "That's one question no-one will ever be able to answer. Anyway, let me get back to what I was saying."

Hetty nodded. "Sorry, Kitty. Please do."

"Well, Miranda, Felix claims, was trapped in a loveless marriage and so she and he used to meet in secret whenever they could and when they last met she told him that soon she would leave Gavin and then they could marry and live happily ever after so to speak."

"Until she got bored with him," grunted Lottie.

"Sorry, Kitty, but how do you know all this?" Hetty suddenly realised it could not have come from the police.

Kitty laughed. "Now this you'll find hard to believe but it appears Felix was in the pub last night. He's booked a room there for a few days, you see. Tommy was in the pub at the time having a drink with Bernie and Sid. They got chatting to Felix and he told them and a few others within earshot what had happened. He said it helped him to talk about it especially to strangers."

"Humph, typical," muttered Debbie, "trust none of us to have been in the pub last night."

Hetty took a sip of her tea. "Hmm, still never mind, please continue, Kitty."

"Yes, please do," Lottie agreed, "because I want to know why Felix thought Benvolio killed Miranda."

"Well, the reason is that Miranda had once told Felix about a partner she'd had before she met and married Gavin Snow; he was a chef named Benvolio Moretti and the day after she left him, he rang her and said that he would be looking for her and, when he found her, would kill her. Apparently she was terrified and instantly changed her mobile number, left Reading where she was staying temporarily with friends and returned to her parents' home in Bodmin. Shortly after that she met Gavin Snow and married him. In her case it wasn't love: it was so that she would be able to change her surname and make it more difficult for Benvolio to trace her."

Hetty shook her head. "I know it's bad to speak ill of the dead but the more I hear of that woman the more I despise her."

"And as much as I'd like to disagree with you, Het, I can't because I also think she was pretty despicable," said Kitty.

186

Debbie frowned. "What I don't understand is why Benvolio threatened to kill Miranda in the first place. I mean surely it wasn't really just because she ditched him. But whatever the reason was, I have to confess that he always struck me as being a decent bloke although I suppose I didn't see him that often."

"I would agree with that but he went down in my estimation when he called me granny." Hetty was indignant.

"But you're more than old enough to be a grandmother," chided Lottie, "you're the same age as me and I have three grandchildren all in their late teens."

"I know that but it was the tone in which he said it that I didn't like."

Debbie laughed. "Pray continue, Kitty before an argument breaks out."

"Okay, but going back to your question, Debbie I'm afraid I can't answer it as I don't know the exact reason for Benvolio wishing to kill Miranda although Felix did say that the police had hinted that when she left him she made off with a substantial amount of money all of which belonged to him. He asked them to clarify their statement but of course they refused."

"Good heavens," spluttered Lottie, "she was a right little money grabber then because she tried to fiddle the insurance company too."

"And would have succeeded had Benvolio not drowned her," Hetty added.

"Sorry, Kitty, we keep interrupting you," said Debbie, "What happened next?"

"Well, at the time when both Gavin and Miranda died, Felix was away at sea."

"In the Navy?"

"No, not in the Navy, Het, on a cruise ship where he worked as a sous chef. Meaning he was frequently away for weeks on end. Anyway, when he got back from the trip he tried to contact

Miranda. He always rang on the landline because she refused to give him her mobile number in case it rang within earshot of Gavin. Of course they knew that it was possible Gavin might answer when he rang the landline and so she insisted if he did that Felix must apologise and say he'd dialled a wrong number."

Lottie tutted. "Duplicitous hussy."

Kitty laughed. "Anyway, when he rang, no-one answered and he tried again and again. Worried that something might be wrong, he drove down to Bodmin to try and find her. It was the next door neighbour who told him they were both dead and that Miranda had killed Gavin. At first he didn't believe it and even when he looked up the case on-line he was still unconvinced. Then his thoughts turned to our chef. You see, as I've already said Miranda had told him about a man with whom she had had a brief fling - Benvolio Moretti who we now know masqueraded as an Italian chef but in reality was born and bred in Liverpool and his real name is Ben Moore."

Hetty chuckled. "Ben Moore. Well, I never. You've got to hand it to the chap he played the part well."

"Yes, we can't take that away from him," Lottie agreed.

"So how did Felix know where to find Benvolio or should I say Ben?" Debbie asked.

"Well, that's quite simple. Knowing that he was a fully qualified chef, Felix Googled the words Benvolio Moretti and Italian chef and it came up with an article announcing that the Crown and Anchor in Pentrillick, Cornwall, was re-opening soon after closure for extension and refurbishment. It said the new licensees, James and Ella Dale, were proud to say they had an Italian chef and that his name was Benvolio Moretti. To establish his whereabouts Felix rang the pub on Monday night and asked on pretence of being an old acquaintance who wanted to surprise his old friend where dear Benvolio was staying. Young Harry answered the phone and told him that Benvolio was staying in one of the caravans on the pub field. Felix asked Harry not to mention the phone call and the rest as they say is history."

"Well, I never," tutted Hetty, "what a to-do."

Lottie appeared confused. "It's probably nothing but I wonder why Miranda's friend Patty didn't tell the police about Felix. I mean, we're pretty sure they questioned her about old boyfriends when trying to find a chap from Liverpool, so why didn't she mention him because surely he could have been a suspect."

Kitty nodded her head. "Funny you should ask that, Lottie, because I've just remembered Tommy saying that someone mentioned Patty last night to Felix and he said he'd never heard of her."

"What," spluttered Hetty, "So it looks like Miranda never told Patty about Felix or vice versa."

"Humph, so she was just using Felix like she did everyone else," said Lottie, "what a good-for-nothing."

Debbie sighed. "Meanwhile, poor James and Ella are now facing the holiday period having just spent a fortune and reopened the pub but have no chef. I feel so sorry for them."

Lottie suddenly looked downcast. "That's true and I was really looking forward to the prawn linguine."

Kitty smiled. "No need because they have a new chef. He's not an Italian Liverpudlian and I've no idea whether or not prawn linguine will be on his menu but he is a good bloke. I don't know his surname but his Christian name is Felix."

"Felix as in the Felix I hit over the head?" gasped Hetty.

Kitty nodded. "Yes, James offered him a job as soon as he heard his story and realised his profession. Tommy said Felix is thrilled to bits because he's been wanting for some time to give up the cruises and work on dry land."

"That's lovely," sang Lottie, "So in a way, all's well that ends well."

Hetty winced. "Maybe but I don't think it would be very wise for me to eat at the Crown and Anchor until the dust settles."

Chapter Twenty-Five

On the last Saturday in July, excited that the big day had finally arrived, villagers were busy in front of their houses titivating their flower beds and attending to their hanging baskets, pots, window boxes and tubs because at two o'clock the judges were due to begin a tour of the village to choose winners in the four categories. And to make sure no-one tried to influence the judge's' decision beforehand, both Justin and Samantha Liddicott-Treen had refused to divulge their identity. The results of the competition were to be announced at seven o'clock in the newly created gardens at the Crown and Anchor.

While most of the competitors were happy with their efforts, things were not so at the Old Bakehouse for outside on the pavement, Bill cried in anguish. "Someone has pinched my tomatoes. Look, all the lovely red ones have gone."

Vicki giggled. "Perhaps someone was hungry."

"Nonsense, it's sabotage," spluttered Bill, "Some cheating no-good saw my baskets as a threat and they've deliberately spoiled my hard work."

"Oh, Dad you're so unlucky," Kate was close to tears.

"Thank you, sweetheart. At least someone shares my pain."

"So what will you do, Dad?" Vicki tried to sound sympathetic but found it difficult to keep a straight face.

Sandra shook her head. "Sadly there's nothing we can do. Not at this late stage."

"Oh, yes there is." Bill grabbed his car keys from the hook by the door and ran round the corner to where his car was parked in Goose Lane. "I'll be back in a jiffy."

Three quarters of an hour later he returned with four packs of cherry tomatoes on vines.

"Oh, Bill, you can't put them in the baskets. The judges will see they're not attached and then we'll be disqualified for cheating."

But Bill was not to be deterred. He took down both baskets and stood them on the dining room table, he then with a piece of cotton carefully tied them to his plants. Once done he mounded up the compost to cover the joins and then hung the baskets back in place.

"See, no-one will ever know."

As they turned to go indoors they saw the postman delivering letters along the main street. Bill, who had been complimented by the postman for his hanging baskets a day or two earlier hung around outside to see if he noticed that the baskets had been tampered with.

"Good morning, postman. Another fine day."

"Good morning, and judgement day too so I hear." The postman glanced up at Bill's baskets, "I'm glad to see your tomatoes are still looking splendid."

Bill beamed with delight. "Thank you, I hope the judges agree."

"Good luck to you," The postman began to walk away and then stopped. "Silly me. I nearly forgot to give you these." He handed over the mail.

As he turned to go indoors, Bill looked through the post. Most was junk mail but at the bottom was an envelope addressed to Mr Z Burton.

"One for you, Zac and the rest for recycling." Bill went out to the utility room where the recycling box was kept.

Sandra, stood in the doorway that led into the hall and held her breath as Zac tore the envelope open. When a huge grin stretched across his face she felt her heart thump wildly.

"They're going to give us a house, Mum. I don't believe it. Oh my god, I must ring Emma." As he dashed from the room to get his phone he gave Sandra a quick hug but in his excitement he didn't see the tears welling in her eyes.

By a quarter to seven a large crowd was assembled in the gardens of the Crown and Anchor. People gathered around the picnic tables, stood in groups and sat on the neatly trimmed grass. The evening was warm and sunny; the atmosphere was jovial and many spoke of the fun they had had preparing for the big day.

Near to the caravan where the chef had once lived, a small platform stood ready for the announcements and at seven o'clock precisely, Samantha and Tristan Liddicott-Treen stepped onto the platform. Tristan spoke into the microphone. "Ladies and Gentlemen, boys and girls, welcome to this the first of hopefully many, Pentrillick in Bloom competition results nights. The judges inform me that they are very impressed by the high standards of work and artistic skills displayed in your entries and that it has been very difficult for them to choose to whom the prizes should go. However, they have made their decisions and I have the results here.

The third prize for small front garden went to Hetty and Lottie. Second to Percy Pickering, known as Pickle, who lived in Hawthorn Road. First prize was awarded to Debbie and Gideon.

Third prize for a large front garden went to a house in St Mary's Avenue. Second prize to Bernie the Boatman and Veronica and first to Kitty and Tommy in Blackberry Way.

The hairdressing salon won best business premises, the post office came second and the fish and chip shop third.

"And," said Tristan, "for the category of tubs, window boxes and hanging baskets the results are as follows – in third place: Natalie and Luke Burleigh."

Sandra clapped loudly, delighted to see her work colleague Natalie and her husband Luke rewarded for the display at their home along the main street.

"Second prize," said Tristan, "goes to Clara Bragg of Church Row."

Clara smiled through gritted teeth as she went to collect her prize money.

"And in first place," Bill squeezed Sandra's hand tightly, "goes to William and Sandra Burton at the Old Bakehouse."

"We did it." Bill picked his wife up and swung her around as they made their way to the platform.

The final prize for the best overall entrant and winner of the first ever Green Fingers Cup was awarded to Tess Dobson. She accepted her prize in a state and shock and made everyone laugh when she admitted that for once in her life she was lost for words.

After the presentations most went into the pub as the wind had suddenly freshened making sitting outdoors a little uncomfortable. Bill and Sandra, delighted at their success celebrated their win with glasses of sparkling wine. As they clinked glasses in a toast, Bill saw that Clara was watching them.

"You alright, Clara?" He chuckled.

She scowled. "So how did you do it?"

"Do what?" Bill was puzzled.

"Win of course. I heard this morning that your tomato plants bore no ripe fruit and so your baskets were devoid of colour. Surely that would have lost you points."

"Then you heard wrong." Bill took his phone from his pocket and showed Clara the pictures he'd taken shortly before the judges came round.

Clara's jaw dropped. "But, I don't understand. I ...."

Bill put down his phone. "It was you, wasn't it? You took my tomatoes in an attempt to wreck my chances."

"But you just said they weren't taken and showed me the pictures as proof."

"Oh bugger."

Sandra laughed.

Clara's eyes flashed. "You're a cheat, Bill Burton."

"It takes one to recognise one," he snapped.

"What do you mean?"

"We saw you at the garden centre putting four hanging baskets into the back of your car. No doubt you'd had them specially made. I'm surprised you didn't win with them though but then perhaps they're past their best now. It takes skill to keep things looking good, you know."

"I bought specially made baskets!" she spluttered. "How dare you?"

"I dare because it's true."

"Prove it." Clara folded her arms; she looked smug.

Sandra passed her phone to Bill who showed Clara the picture taken at the garden centre.

The two glared at each other, daggers drawn and then Bill laughed. "Care to join for a drink?"

Clara bit her bottom lip and then offered her hand for Bill to shake.

Bill took it, "I'm not one to bear a grudge," he said, "and at the end of the day I won anyway, so there."

Sandra coughed. "We won, Bill. You did the baskets, but I did the tubs and window boxes."

Clara smiled. "Yes, and if I'm perfectly honest, Sandra, the prize was well deserved."

Outside the Crown and Anchor, a taxi pulled up in the new car park. From the driver's seat leapt Elliot Harris who opened the back door and helped Betsy Triggs step down onto the tarmac. He locked the vehicle; she then took his arm and he escorted her inside the pub. As they emerged through the door several heads turned and Betsy sensed her companion's unease. "Hold your head up high, Elliot," she commanded, "and smile. These are good people and if you play your cards right you will earn their trust and they will become your friends."

As he looked around for an empty chair, Lottie sprang to her feet. "Over here, Elliot, there's room for the two of you here if we all otch up."

"If you all what?" Elliot scratched his head.

"Otch up. It means move up, you know, to make more room."

"Betsy laughed as she sat. "I've never heard that one before. It's clearly not Cornish."

"No, it's a bit of good old Northamptonshire dialect. Our mum said it frequently, didn't she, Het?"

"She certainly did m'duck."

Baffled by the weird conversation Elliot went to the bar to buy a round of drinks, but with a smile on his lips. The ice had been broken.

Later in the evening, when he finished work, Felix the new chef emerged from the kitchen and took a seat at the end of the bar where James, grateful for him having come to their rescue, handed him a pint of cider. Hetty standing further along the bar watched as he took several sips. When it was her turn to be served she ordered drinks for herself, her sister and their friends. "And please, James, put one in for your new chef. I think after what happened last week I owe it to him."

With refilled glasses on a tray, Hetty returned to the table by the fireplace and passed around the drinks. She then sat down. As she placed her handbag on the floor by her feet, she saw Felix walking in her direction.

"Cheers," he said.

"No hard feelings?" she nervously asked.

He shook his head. "None at all. Had I been in your position then I probably would have done the same thing."

Feeling a great sense of relief, Hetty raised her glass and clinked it against his pint of cider. "Then cheers and I hope you'll be very happy here."

"I'm sure I will. As they say it's an ill wind and so forth."

After a brief chat with Norman who was delighted to report the sale of his house and the purchase of a house on the new estate were going well, Bill went to look for Sandra but she was nowhere to be found. Realising that she might have gone outside for a breath of fresh air he went out into the gardens to find her. On a picnic table bench he saw her sitting alone looking up at the stars. His heart skipped a beat; she looked so small, so lonely. With haste he walked in her direction and then sat down by her side. He took her hand. "It's been an emotional day for you, hasn't it? I mean learning Zac's going and then winning first prize."

She nodded. "It has and in a way one compensates for the other. I'll be alright tomorrow when I've got used to the idea of Zac going." She looked down at her empty glass, "and wine is inclined to make me feel maudlin."

"Bill put his arm around her shoulders and pulled her close. "Zac's really happy and so is Emma. Surely that's the main thing."

"Yes, it is I know. It's just that I'll miss him so much. He was our first born and he's our only son. I thought it was hard all those years ago when he started school but this is a hundred times worse." Tears streamed down her face.

Bill kissed her hair. "You've still got me. I'm not going anywhere."

"Promise?"

"Of course," Bill stood up, "Come on, dry those pretty eyes and let's go back indoors."

Once in the pub, Sandra went to the Ladies to touch up her make-up while Bill went to the bar for more drinks.

Inside the Ladies, looking into a mirror while brushing her hair was Emma. Emma turned when she saw Sandra's red eyes. She put down the hairbrush and gave her a hug. "Zac told me that his dad said you were tearful this morning but Zac was too excited to notice. You know you'll always be welcome to visit us and I'm sure that Zac will pop home often. Please don't be upset."

Sandra kissed Emma on the cheek. "Thank you and I know you'll look after him. I think it all came as a bit of shock. I didn't expect you'd hear for a while, you see." She opened her handbag and took out her powder compact.

"Nor did I, if I'm honest." Emma finished brushing her hair. The two then went back out into the bar with arms linked and walked over towards the French doors where Zac was talking to Bill. Bill handed her a glass of wine.

Sandra raised her glass. "Cheers, and now I think it's time we did a little more celebrating and then tomorrow perhaps we can go up to the new estate and peep in the downstairs windows of your new home."

As the pub rocked to nineteen sixties music, a police car drove along the main street and pulled up by the kerb outside the Old Bakehouse. The petite female police officer in the front passenger seat stepped from the car and knocked on the yellow front door. There was no answer. She knocked again. Still no answer. She turned to the car and spoke to her colleague in the driver's seat who was looking at his reflection in the rear view mirror, for having Goggled Jason King after his visit to Primrose Cottage, the officer had grown a droopy moustache. "Looks like there's no-one home."

"I suppose they're at the pub for the results night for the flower thing." He twisted the mirror back into place.

"Yeah, so what shall I do?"

"Leave it outside the door I suppose. They'll know what it is because the guvnor told him he'd send it back."

"But someone might nick it."

"No, I shouldn't think so. Folks around here are pretty honest."

"You're kidding, right?"

"Yeah, alright then, I'll correct that. Most folks around here are pretty honest."

From the back seat of the car the police officer took a large polythene bag containing Bill's original hanging basket. "It looks a bit sad."

"So would you if you'd been through the same ordeal as that has."

Seeing there was nowhere else to put it, she dropped the bag on the doorstep and then climbed back into the car. "Hopefully things will be a bit quieter here now all the recent crimes have been solved."

"The driver started the engine. "Maybe but I wouldn't hold your breath."

THE END

198